PROTECTING Rachael

Lewis Security Agency Book 1

Teresa Reitnauer

Copyright © 2023 **Teresa Reitnauer**

All rights reserved. No part of this publication may be reproduced, distributed, or transmitted in any form or by any means, including photocopying, recording, or other electronic or mechanical methods, without the prior written permission of the publisher, except in the case of brief quotations embodied in critical reviews and certain other noncommercial uses permitted by copyright law. For permission requests, write to the publisher, addressed "Attention: Book Rights and Permission," at the address below.

Published in the United States of America

ISBN 978-1-961507-03-6 (SC)
ISBN 978-1-961507-01-2 (HC)
ISBN 978-1-961507-02-9 (Ebook)

Teresa Reitnauer
222 West 6th Street
Suite 400, San Pedro, CA, 90731
tsreitnauer@gmail.com

Ordering Information and Rights Permission:

Quantity sales. Special discounts might be available on quantity purchases by corporations, associations, and others. For details, contact the publisher at the address above.

For Book Rights Adaptation and other Rights Permission. Call us at toll-free 1-888-945-8513 or send us an email at admin@stellarliterary.com.

Contents

Chapter 1 1
Chapter 2 5
Chapter 3 8
Chapter 4 15
Chapter 5 23
Chapter 6 27
Chapter 7 31
Chapter 8 37
Chapter 9 42
Chapter 10 43
Chapter 11 45
Chapter 12 51
Chapter 13 54
Chapter 14 57
Chapter 15 60
Chapter 16 66
Chapter 17 71
Chapter 18 77
Chapter 19 80
Chapter 20 84
Chapter 21 86
Chapter 22 91
Chapter 23 93
Chapter 24 99
Chapter 25 103
Chapter 26 109
Chapter 27 113
Chapter 28 121
Epilogue 123

Chapter 1

Beep! Rachael checked the ID for the incoming message. Another unknown caller. Replacing the phone in her blazer pocket, she continued into the restaurant for her lunch meeting with her agent.

"Hello, Rachael. How's it going?" Masie, the hostess at Sylvia Greens, asked. Rachael and her agent met at Sylvia's for their monthly lunch meetings, and Masie acknowledged them by name each time.

"Doing well. Is Gretchen here? I'm a little early."

"No worries. Gretchen reserved a table in the back to get away from the lunch crowd."

Rachael followed Masie through the noisy, bustling dining room to a smaller, empty room. "I'll send Gretchen back when she arrives."

"Thanks."

Rachael sat at the same time Gretchen hurried in with her assistant, Lily, in tow. "I'm sorry I'm late. I had a last minute phone call that couldn't be put off. A new author had some questions about her book deal."

"You're not late. I arrived a couple of minutes ago. Hello, Lily."

"Hi."

"I'm anxious about this book tour." Rachael unwrapped her silverware with shaking hands and the fork fell to the floor.

"Rachael, you've nothing to worry about. Everything is all set up." Gretchen patted her hand. "Three book signings and two readings in four cities, ending here in Turtle Cove. I made the reservations myself for the hotel stays. Since this is your first tour, I'm sending Lily with you to help navigate the events."

"I couldn't impose on either of you." Turning to Gretchen, she said, "You need Lily to help you with your day-to-day appointments. I'll manage on my own."

"You'll be gone a week. I can handle any crisis that occurs. I want you to have support this first time out. It's settled. Now, let's order lunch." Rachael knew once Gretchen made up her mind, it's a done deal.

An hour later, the three women exited the restaurant and walked to their cars. "Since the three other cities you're visiting are within 100 miles, do you mind if Lily rides with you?" Gretchen asked. "That way, you can organize how you want things to proceed."

"That would be great. If I totally flub up on my first signing, Lily can help steer me in the right direction."

"You'll do fine," reassured Lily, handing a piece of paper to Rachael. "Here's a copy of the itinerary in case you misplaced the original."

"Thanks, but I have it on my tablet. Oh, by the way, I noticed the signs in Hector's Book Corner windows advertising the signing. They turned out awesome. I broke out in goosebumps reading my name on the poster. The display of my books stood off to the right as you enter the door."

"That's great. I'll arrive at Hector's ahead of time to make sure everything is in order and remain through the signing," announced Gretchen.

"Well Lily, are you ready to hit the road? If we leave now, we have time to check into the hotel and freshen up before the book signing this evening."

"I need to retrieve my suitcase from Gretchen's car." Gretchen popped the truck open for Lily.

After Lily loaded her bag into Rachael's car, Gretchen said, "Drive safely and see you in a week at Hector's."

"Okay."

"Bye." Lily and Rachael responded at the same time and got into Rachael's car.

Once on the road, Rachael's phone beeped again. Since she was driving, she ignored it.

"Do you want me to check who that was for you?" asked Lily.

"No. I'll check it at the hotel. I've been receiving a lot of strange messages from an unknown person. That was probably another one."

Two hours later, Rachael drove into the crowded hotel parking lot, dropped Lily off at the front door, and parked the car. She rolled both suitcases to the front desk, checking out the ornate sculpture standing in the center of lobby as she passed by. Lily handed Rachael her key card, and they headed to the room.

Upon entering, Lily said, "Wow! What a beautiful bouquet of flowers. Perhaps Gretchen sent them to kick off your tour."

Checking the nondescript card, Rachael rolled her eyes. "They're not from Gretchen. It's not signed."

"What does it say?"

"Good Luck on tour! I'm with you always."

"That's creepy since it's not signed. Any idea who sent them?"

"Not a clue." Rachael shrugged her shoulders. "Let's get ready for the book signing."

An hour later, they strolled into Book Haven. The smell of books and coffee relaxed Rachael. It felt like home. A small group of people surrounded a table set up for her use. A middle-aged woman introduced herself as the manager of the store. After directing them to the counter for coffee and cookies, the manager clapped her hands.

"Our special guest has arrived. We'll start in fifteen minutes."

Taking a deep breath, Rachael squeezed Lily's forearm and made her way to the table. Before sitting, she said, "Thank you all for coming. I hope you enjoy my book. I would love to hear any feedback, positive or negative. My email is listed on the final page." She enjoyed talking to people about her books. Time flew and the crowd thinned.

When no one else stood at her table, Lily said, "Great job. I've heard nothing but complements about your writing. Gretchen and I believe you have a bestseller on your hands."

"I'm just glad people enjoy reading it." Turning to the manager, "Thank you for hosting the book signing. You have a charming book store. I could spend hours in here reading."

"It was my pleasure to host this signing. Now more people know about my little slice of heaven," replied the manager.

The next two stops went about the same. A bouquet of flowers at each hotel. Rachael told Lily to return them to the front desk to be enjoyed by all the guests. Rachael shut off her phone, knowing that if her agent needed her, Gretchen would call Lily. The tight muscles and dull ache came from the unending vibrations from incoming texts. Thankfully, nothing out of the ordinary happened at the events planned.

On the final leg of the tour back to Turtle Cove, Lily said, "You can drop me off at the office before the reading at the library. Then I'll see you at Hector's with Gretchen."

"Thanks for going and calming me down when those stupid flowers kept showing up."

"No problem. Everyone has an obsessed fan. I think you should change your phone number to stop the texts."

"Thanks. I'll do that tomorrow as I decompress from the trip." Arriving in front of the agent's office, she added, "See you at Hector's."

Chapter 2

Strolling into Hector's Book Corner thirty minutes ahead of schedule, Rachael found Lily and Gretchen by the area set up for her. A pile of books sat on the table and a carton behind. She greeted the women as she pulled her pens out of her bag, placing them on the table.

"How are you holding up?" asked Gretchen. "Lily told me about the flowers and texts."

Rachael drank a sip of water before answering, "A little stressed, but Lily was a life saver. Thanks again for sending her with me." She took her seat and waited for the first customer.

4:00 p.m. on the dot, the first customer wandered to the table. As Rachael was signing the book, more people formed a line. Out of the corner of her eye, she saw a clerk hanging around. Several people started asking questions about her writing, but the clerk shuffled them on.

With a lull in customers wanting their books signed, Rachael turned to the clerk. "I know you think you are helping. However, I don't need your assistance."

"It's my job to move the people along," he insisted.

Rachael couldn't respond because more people arrived to have their books signed. The clerk told them to move on before they could speak to Rachael. She grimaced every time he opened his mouth.

Noticing the problem, Lily intervened. "Chet, please leave the customers alone. I'll assist Ms. Simmons. We don't need you."

"I can help. There's a lot of people taking valuable time."

"Ms. Simmons enjoys talking to her readers. Please leave now before I call the manager over here."

Huffing, Chet stomped off to the back of the store.

"Thank you, Lily. He was getting on my nerves." Rachael sighed and rolled her shoulders before continuing.

"You can relax and have fun talking."

At the end of the event, all the books had been sold and signed. Rachael picked up her pens and tossed her empty bottle in the recycle bin. As she headed toward Gretchen, the clerk came back out and kept interrupting, asking her out for coffee. He refused to take no for an answer. He scowled at her when she said, "Enough. You have made me and my fans uncomfortable. Please keep your distance." She turned and walked out with the other two ladies.

2 days later

Rachael planned the tour in her writing schedule, but the stress from the last signing put her behind. She couldn't afford any interruptions. Her phone started whistling. She answered and nobody responded, but she could hear breathing. "Hello, is anyone there?" Silence greeted her, so she clicked the end button.

This happened three more times. Ready for a lunch break, Rachael headed toward the door. Her phone started again. Leaving it on the counter, she strode out.

An hour later, she entered her studio apartment only to hear the whistling tone of her phone. The unknown ID appeared. She muted the phone and went back to work. Several hours later, she finished for the day and copied her work on a thumb drive. She checked her phone for anything important she might have missed. Seeing three messages from the unknown caller, she tossed the phone aside.

She planned to meet her best friend in the world, Melissa Dressler, for a girl's night out. She dressed in a slinky, black dress and stiletto heels. Leaving the studio, she grabbed her phone and it lit up in her hand. Running late, she thought it might be Melissa.

After answering, she heard the heavy breathing. She hung up, shoved the phone into her purse, and left to meet her friend.

Around midnight, Rachael stumbled home. Taking her phone out to check, it lit up again. She checked the ID: Unknown. Ignoring it, she went to bed.

As each day passed, bouquets of flowers appeared at her door with no note. The anonymous calls continued. She left her phone on, but muted, in case her agent called. From the corner of her eye, she could see the light from the phone calls. She was on a tight deadline, and these calls were disturbing her concentration.

After a few days, she couldn't take it anymore. She packed a few things along with her computer and left her sanctuary. The constant phone calls and flowers creeped her out. Rachael left to find another place to write, hoping to finish her manuscript.

Chapter 3

The unknown caller hadn't seen or heard Rachael for three days. She wasn't answering the calls anymore. On the rare occasion she did, she would hang up. He put a tracker on her phone the last time she left it at the apartment. He needed to find her, to know she was all right. He needed to protect her, her friends didn't care about the people bothering her. Keeping her safe became a necessity for him. Ever since he saw the poster hanging in the windows, he felt an immediate connection to her. He found out where she lived and her book tour schedule. He placed cameras at her studio to watch for trouble. He sent flowers to each of the hotels she stayed at to show her how much he cared for her. Didn't she realize they belonged together, because they were soul mates? That's the reason for all the flowers and phone calls. "What's this?" he saw movement at the door. "Yeah! It's her."

Struggling to focus at the quaint little coffee shop she found, Rachael placed her fingers in her hair and pulled. She had work to do and couldn't concentrate with all the customers coming and going. The studio was her writing haven. That is until her book tour ended. The stupid calls made her feel anxious and out of sync with her creativity. She needed to go back to the beautiful space she found through a fellow colleague. Decision made, she collected her laptop and papers.

Exiting the shop, Rachael seized a moment to take a deep breath and enjoy the sun on her face before heading back to the hotel to pick up her personal belongings. Parking her car a few blocks from her oasis, she hiked the short distance, stopping at the corner store for some groceries.

At the register, she asked the clerk, "Anything unusual happening around the area, Chuck?" She wanted to see if her persistent caller was harassing anyone else. Everyone talked to Chuck.

"Nothing out of the ordinary. I haven't seen you around in a couple of days. Everything all right?"

"Yeah, I had some personal issues and spent a few days away. I'm heading back to finish my book."

"Well, happy writing, Rachael."

"Thanks. Have a great day," said Rachael, heading out the door.

A few minutes later, she arrived at the building that host places for all artistic types. Seeing her arms full, a fellow writer held the door to allow her to enter with no fuss. She didn't know his name but had seen him around the building. Thanking him, she took the stairs to the second floor and managed to pull her keys out. Struggling with the groceries and the laptop bag to unlocked the door, the last thing she wanted to hear was the whistling tune of her cell phone. It couldn't be hers because the muted phone sat in her back pocket. Shaking her head to clear it, she opened her door.

Closing the door with her foot, relief flooded her that there were no flowers in the hall. When she gazed around her charming room, she let out a big sigh. Maybe things were back to normal. Home at last, she loved this place. Dropping her duffle bag on the floor and her laptop bag into the armchair, she ambled into her cute kitchenette and put the groceries away. On the other side of the room stood a folding screen that set off her bed and the bathroom. Pulling her phone out for a quick glance, she tossed it on the counter. More missed calls from unknown caller.

At first, the calls irritated Rachael, but she thought they would stop at some point. As the pestering calls continued, she grew more anxious. Rachael took note they came when she arrived or left. It felt like someone was watching her. If she stayed in for a long period of time, the calls would start again. Her phone connected her to Gretchen. She had no choice but to check the dang thing when it rang, so those strange incidents frayed her nerves. Her focus strayed away from her book.

She took a moment to stare out the windows, loving how the sunshine streamed through the giant panes all along the outside wall. The room always felt warm and cheerful. She set up a desk with her computer facing the windows to get the best views.

However, since these calls started, her once pleasant unit, where she did her best work, had become a place she tried to avoid. Staying away made her creativity sink lower than ever before.

Gathering herself and taking a few deep breaths, Rachael decided to thwart the interrupts. Her agent wanted to see the current book finished by the end of the month. She dialed Gretchen.

"Hello, Rachael. Tell me the book is in my inbox."

"Sorry, Gretchen. I have been plagued by anonymous phone calls. I'm having a hard time focusing."

"Turn the damn phone off and concentrate on the book. If anything urgent comes up, I will send Lily over to let you know. You have two weeks to get me the manuscript."

With slumping shoulders, she replied, "Okay, okay. I'll get started right away. I promise it won't be late." Rachael was three quarters done. However, the ending was causing her trouble. Some serious writing time had to be put in to get it completed.

Rachael made some coffee and set her laptop up to get started. Picking up the phone to shut it down, it lit up in her hand. With her mind focused on her ending scene, Rachael answered without checking the ID.

"Hello." She froze when the only sound heard was the breathing. A heavy breathing, as though the caller had been exercising.

"Where have you been the last few days?" the raspy voice shouted.

Rachael started to tremble. "What do you want? Why do you keep calling and not say anything?" she cried into the phone. The evil sounding voice scared her more than the breathing. The caller knew she'd avoided the unit for several days. The feeling of being watched must be correct. Her hand holding the phone shook.

"I know your every move. You can't avoid me. We're connected," roared the eerie voice.

"Just leave me alone. Stop calling me." Frightened more than a little, Rachael disconnected the call, turned it off, and left it on the counter.

The coffee had finished brewing, so she poured herself a cup and added some cream. Putting the creepy call out of her mind, she sat at her desk and opened her manuscript.

With so many emotions running through her, it was difficult getting started. After a few deep breaths, her concentration returned. The words started flowing, making good progress. At this pace, she'd complete the book in plenty of time to meet her deadline.

Her stomach started growling. Needing a break, Rachael stood and observed the beautiful colors of the sky before the sun's rays disappeared. The excitement within her inspired her to take a stroll to the deli down at the corner. Some fresh air and a good sub would help clear her mind to complete her task. Making sure to save her work, she headed toward the door and glanced at her phone on the counter. She left it and moved out the door.

Rachael returned an hour later, rejuvenated and eager to continue. As she approach the door, a bouquet of dead wilted flowers leaned against it. Her good mood refused to let them bother her as she tossed them in the trash once she entered her studio.

Expecting to work late, she brewed another pot of coffee to get her through. Her fingers danced across the keyboard. She took short breaks to refill her coffee cup and stretch her legs. Around midnight, she typed "The End". She yawned and decided to get some sleep before editing her work. A full-size bed behind a screen beckoned her. Exhausted but please, she copied her book onto the thumb drive and put it in her computer bag.

Slipping on a loose shirt and shorts that she slept in, she checked her phone again and noticed another ten missed calls from the same ID. The caller was relentless. There were also two messages. They were doubtless more heavy breathing, but she'd check just in case. Since it was late, it could wait until the next day.

The next morning, Rachael did her daily stretching routine. Seeing the sunny day, she decided a good long walk would help center her before the final editing. She grabbed her fanny pack and put the thumb drive in it. She picked up her phone to take for any emergency. With it on mute, it wouldn't disturb the quiet, natural setting she would be enjoying. As she was leaving, her phone lit up in her hand.

Checking the ID, she hit ignore, put it in her pack, and strolled out the door. Listening to music through her ear buds connected to her MP3, she set out on a steady pace. As she trekked around the trail, she smiled at the running squirrels, flying birds, and the leaves swaying in the slight breeze. Nature had a way of calming her nerves.

The rambling path behind the building was a three mile loop. Long enough to give her exercise and fresh air to clear her mind. The route went through a grove of trees with flowering bushes scattered throughout. The hike relaxed and stimulated Rachael.

At the end of her hike, she slipped into the deli for a smoothie to cool down. It was a crisp morning, but striding briskly still warmed a person up. She didn't rush back, sitting at one of the outdoor tables in front of the deli. Taking note of her surroundings gave Rachael ideas for her stories. She kept a little notebook in her fanny pack to jot things down that popped in her head.

Finishing her smoothie, she checked her phone. Sure enough, there were more missed calls from Unknown "Will he ever give up?" she asked herself. Rachael sauntered back to her studio.

Edging closer to her home, the open door stopped her in her tracks. She knew she'd locked it. She remembered using the key on the dead bolt. She hesitantly stepped in and gasped at the damage done to her place. The TV was smashed and the laptop destroyed. Thankfully, she'd backed up her book on the thumb drive and took it with her. She backed up her work after every session, not taking any chances of losing her progress. The screen blocking her bed was broken. Her bed was brutally slashed, and the pillows were ripped apart. Her clothes were shredded and thrown about. The dead flowers from her trash were tossed everywhere. She ran like the devil was at her back into the hall and called 9-1-1.

When she finished the call, she slid down the wall and buried her head in her hands. Rachael couldn't believe someone would do something so cruel. Why? What had she done to deserve it? Her phone lit up in her lap. With tears in her eyes, she clicked accept and got her answer.

"You can't just ignore my calls!" the nasty voice bellowed. "I told you we are connected! You made me angry, and you got what you deserved," the voice continued ranting.

"Stop. You had no right! I'm telling the police everything. They'll catch you and send you to jail. I've had enough." With that, Rachael hung up the phone and gave it a heave. It slid down the hall a few doors down and stopped. Just then, the police came up the stairs.

Taking in the scene, an officer asked, "Are you all right, miss?" Seeing how distraught she looked, he picked up her phone as he passed by it. Handing it back to her, he continued in a gentle tone, "What happened here?"

Rachael stood up when the officer handed her the phone. "Someone broke into my place and destroyed everything!" Rachael shouted. "Just look at this mess!" She pointed inside the door with shaking hands.

"Was anything taken? Anything of value?" the officer asked, trying to calm her down before she became hysterical.

"No, just ruined," Rachael responded with slumped shoulders.

"Has anything else been going on?" the other officer inquired.

"Yes, strange calls with heavy breathing. Mostly, they come when I go in or out. Also, bouquets of flowers with no notes left by my door. This has been going on for a couple of weeks. I left for a few days, because I got tired of everything. The calls continued even when I was gone. I'm a writer, and I do my best work here, so I came back yesterday. When the next call came in, he spoke saying something about knowing my every move, and that we're connected, whatever that means." Rachael threw up her hand in despair. She continued, "It was an eerie, creepy voice. Nobody I recognized. I shut my phone off and continued writing. This morning, I went for a hike around the park. When I returned, this is what I found. Just before you came, he called again. He was irate because I ignored him. He said I deserved this. I don't know who this person is. I don't know anything." Out of steam, Rachael wilted back to the floor.

The police officers went in to check out the space, careful not to touch anything.

Seeing the destruction, they called the crime scene unit to pick up any clues. Back in the hall, an officer asked, "Can we call someone for you?" She shook her head, tears streaming down her face.

Her phone lit up again. Answering it, she shouted, "How dare you violate my home!"

"Uh, Rachael, what are you talking about? It's me, Melissa," said the soothing familiar voice.

"Oh, Melissa. I'm sorry. I've had the worst morning. Someone broke into my home and trashed the place. I've been getting strange phone calls and secretive bouquets of flowers left by my door. I'm down right terrified!" Rachael explained to her friend.

"Oh, honey. I'll be there in a few minutes."

"Thank you. That'd be great." Disconnecting the call, Rachael turned to the officers. "Can I leave now?"

"Sure. Let me have your number and have our tech team try to trace the calls." After exchanging numbers, she waited outside her building for Melissa.

Chapter 4

In the quiet empty room, Captain Randall Lewis waited for his final appointment with Dr. Stevenson. His duffle bag sat on the floor next to him. The room provided a calm place where nothing could cause any of the embarrassing nervousness he felt around loud noises.

Lewis had spent ten years in the service with two tours in Afghanistan. At the end of this last required session, his discharge out of the Marines became final. He didn't pass his physical or psychological assessment. A road side bomb made sure of that. He was blown clear of the wreckage and knocked unconscious. His fellow comrades were not so lucky. When he came to, he was in a helicopter transporting him to Bagram Air Force Base, in Germany, for medical care. After several weeks, he arrived stateside.

This last session with the psychiatrist was a requirement before leaving the hospital. He arranged for a taxi to arrive in an hour to pick him up. The military sent him to a VA clinic close to his mother's place. With nothing to concentrate on, his mind drifted off to his last mission. Everyone was joking, always keeping a watch out for snipers or other hazards. Unfortunately, buried land mines are hard to detect.

"Captain Lewis, please come in." Dr. Emily Stevenson spoke softly, trying not to startle him. Shaking the images from his mind, he followed the doctor into her office. His pronounced limp, souvenir from the explosion, made walking difficult. His fighting days were over, and he was angry. He loved being a Marine, loved fighting for his country. He pushed and pushed in rehab to get back into top form, but his leg just wouldn't cooperate. The shrapnel that pierced his leg tore some muscles and nerves that would never heal enough to allow him to pass the physical.

"How are you today?" asked Dr. Stevenson.

"How do you think I am, Doc? I'm being forced out. Being a Marine is all I know. What do I do now?" Slapping his leg, he continued, "I have this stupid limp and every loud noise makes me dive for cover. I avoid people for fear of having a break down. I'm not fit to be a man, much less a Marine," Lewis lashed out.

"Are you still having the nightmares?"

"Yes!" Ever since regaining consciousness at the hospital, he would have recurring nightmares of the explosion. They would come at any time of the day, sleeping or awake. He never saw the actual site, but he'd seen pictures of the results of the bomb. How he was blown from the Humvee was beyond his recollection. Why did he survive when his buddies didn't? His friends had families. He was the one single man in the Humvee. He would have traded places with any of the others.

They diagnosed his condition as survivor's guilt along with Post-Traumatic Stress Disorder (PTSD). They gave him anti-anxiety pills to help him when things got rough. He hated to be dependent on medications to live his life. He wished he'd been killed in the explosion.

He could see Dr. Stevenson's lips moving but nothing penetrated his brain. Mention of the nightmares brought everything to the forefront. That horrible day replayed in his mind again.

The doctor could tell Randall was struggling. "Captain Lewis!" she shouted to get his attention, bringing him back to the present.

"What?" asked Lewis, shaking his head to dispel the images of the carnage.

"I'd like to continue seeing you after you leave the clinic. There're still some issues that need to be worked on. I hope you'll continue on with therapy," she suggested.

"Listen, Doc, I appreciated what you're trying to do. Right now, I want to get away from all the noise and people. I need to wrap my head around leaving the Marines and try to decide what to do next," he replied, staring straight at the doctor.

"I —"she started.

Randall interrupted her, "This is what I want. Thank you for your help, but I need to figure this out on my own. After all, it is my life we are talking about."

"Okay. Here's my number if you need to talk to someone." She handed him a business card and shook his hand. "Good luck, Captain Lewis," she proclaimed.

"It's just Randall Lewis now, Doc. Thanks again for everything." With that said, Lewis got up, slid his duffle bag on his shoulder, and limped out of the office. Flipping the card between his hands, his first instinct was to toss it in the trash container by the door, but he shoved it into his pocket. Maybe he might need it later.

As he strolled out of the hospital, he noticed a familiar car waiting at the curved drive at the entrance. Lewis continued toward the car as the driver got out.

"Hello, Randall," said the elder gentleman in uniform. "Would you like a lift?"

"Hey Dad, what are you doing here?"

"Your mother told me you were getting out today, and I thought I would come to see if you needed a ride. I know I'm the last person you expected to see right now, but I want to help out in any way I can," declared Colonel Robert Lewis.

Randall was astonished. His mom and dad separated the summer before he started high school. They never divorced, but his dad never came back again. Apparently, the colonel still talked to his estranged wife, which surprised the heck out of Randall. He hadn't talked to his dad since joining the Corps. Much to Randall's relief, their paths never crossed, until now.

"I don't want to trouble you, Dad," Randall admitted. His dad never had time before, why now?

"I'm sorry I've not come before now. I just arrived stateside and heard from your mother what happened. I read the briefing from the accident. No one informed me," stuttered Robert.

"Don't sweat it, Dad. I didn't expect you to come," he sneered. "Here comes the cab I called. Thanks for the offer."

"Randall, please stop. Let me drive you to your mother's. I'd like to talk to you. I'll pay the cab his fare that he'd have gotten. Just please, hear me out," his dad pleaded, hoping his son would give him a chance.

Randall didn't want to argue here, so he agreed to go with his dad. He watched the colonel go over to the cab, hand him some money, and sent him on his way. Randall opened the back door and threw his duffel in. He took his seat on the passenger side and waited for his dad.

This would be the first time he'd seen his mom in ten years. Whenever he took leave, he always went someplace different around where he was stationed. He should've made the effort to see her. He wrote letters, just never visited, even though she asked a thousand times. It wasn't home, it was his mom's house.

His dad got into the car and started it. He eased through the parking lot and continued out onto the main road. His mom moved into a new house when Randall enlisted. He'd never seen it, but she wrote about how she decorated it and sent pictures. He knew it was a short distance from the clinic, so it shouldn't get too awkward between his dad and him.

The colonel left when he started high school and never came back. For several nights, Randall heard his mother crying in her room. He knew his mom had an affair, but his dad never gave her a second chance.

He had missed his dad, but Robert hurt them with his leaving and lack of communication. Randall stared out the window as his thoughts continued. As far as he knew, they never divorced. One day, he noticed a bank statement on the table and saw his father had money deposited into their joint account. He wondered how his mother afforded staying in their house. He always pondered where the colonel was stationed, but never brought the subject up. His mom had been hurt enough.

"Hey, Dad. You said you wanted to talk, so let's talk," his son exclaimed, ending the silence.

"Son, I don't know where to begin. I thought about this meeting for a long time. I never meant to hurt you. There were times I tried to call, but as soon as the phone started ringing, I hung up. I felt you were better off without me in your life. Even though the problem was between your mother and me, you got the worst of it, and I'm sorry. I've retired from the Corps. I want to see if your mother and I can work out our problems.

"I'd like to be around for you, if you'll let me. I'll understand if you don't. Just remember, I'm here for you." Robert's voice cracked and he gripped the steering wheel so tight his knuckles turned white.

"Thanks, Dad. I wish you luck with Mom though. She's become very independent since I left for the Marines. As for me, I just need some alone time to adjust. I'll visit for a short time with Mom, but I'm going to find someplace quiet to straighten out my head," he explained.

"Well, just remember, you do have family and friends that care. Reach out to them when you need to. Don't let your stubborn pride get you as miserable as mine has gotten me."

Randall smirked but continued to stare out the windows. They were turning onto his mom's street. When his dad parked in front of the house, they both released a puff of air.

"Well, let's get you inside, so your mother can see we made it without hurting one another. She was worried about your reaction with me picking you up," Robert said with a little chuckle.

They got out of the car and headed up the pathway to the front door. Both hesitated, not feeling they had the right to just walk in, so Randall knocked. Claire Lewis answered the door saying, "You don't have to knock. You're my son and always welcome to come right in." She pulled him in the house and gave him a big hug. Robert stayed at the door, letting mother and son have their reunion. Stepping back from her son, Claire turned and invited him in. He entered in and shut the door. Randall noticed the uneasiness between his parents. He hoped things worked out for them.

Randall was happy to see his mother again. "Mom, it is good to see you. I'm so sorry I never came to visit." He gave her another big hug, whispering in her ear, "I missed you."

Claire was misty-eyed. "Well, you two come in and make yourself comfortable. Would you like anything?" They both shook their heads and headed into the living room. "I hope you'll stay here, Randall. I made up the spare room, just in case," she offered.

"I may stay a day or two, but as I told Dad, I'm going to go someplace quiet and decide what's the next chapter." At the crestfallen look on his mother's face, he regretted his visit would be short.

He'd come back once he had a clearer idea of his future. The sadness she displayed cut right through him.

"You can stay here as long as you want. I'm just so glad to see you. I guess your dad told you we're going to try to work things out. I know I made mistakes, and I'm sorry how things transpired. My actions hurt both of you."

To change the sticky subject, Randall sniffed and said, "Something smells delicious."

"Oh, I hope you're hungry. I fixed your favorite, lasagna. Your thin body tells me you could use a good home cooked meal. Let me go check on things. I'll be right back." She hurried to the kitchen, leaving son and father alone.

"I hope you two can find a way to be together."

"It'll be a tough go, but it seems we want the same outcome. I never gave us a chance before, and that is on me. I'm going to try my best this time." Robert's voice crackled.

A loud crash came from the kitchen. Randall fell to the ground and covered his head. He started hyperventilating. He saw his father glance at him and go to the kitchen. He was thankful to be left alone. He slowed his breathing and sat back up on the sofa. He fought to not go back to that horrible place in his mind. He should just leave. He didn't want to trouble his parents with his condition. Then again, his mother was so excited to see him, he couldn't hurt her anymore.

He was sitting on the couch, hanging his head. His dad sat next to him and squeezed his shoulder. "Your mom had a little problem in the kitchen. The lasagna pan jumped out of her hands and ended on the floor. All is not lost, we ordered pizza. If I remember correctly, you like everything but the kitchen sink on it," he said with a slight laugh.

Randall gave a weak smile in return. "I want to thank you, Dad, for not making a big deal about what happened. I know you noticed it. I have trouble with loud noises and being around lots of people.

"Thanks for keeping Mom occupied. The last thing I need is for her to linger over me. I'll stay tonight, but I need to find someplace where I can be alone. I hope you and Mom understand. Anyway, you two need some time alone to work on your marriage," he said with a slight grin on his face.

"Yes, I knew what was happening. I also explained it to your mother. I can't promise she won't hover, because she loves you. I'm sure she'll do her best. Didn't you have a friend that had a cabin on a lake somewhere not too far?"

"That's right. Tom Malone's parents have a nice secluded cabin on a lake. I'll give him a call tomorrow and asked him about the possibility of using it. Thanks for reminding me."

"Here's the pizza," exclaimed Claire. She set it on the coffee table. "I'll get some paper plates and napkins. What would you like to drink?" Robert asked for a beer and Randall said a soda.

After she went into the kitchen, Randall noticed his dad's raised brow.

"You used to love your beer."

"With the medications I'm currently taking, I'm staying away from alcohol. Believe me, I'd love to have a good cold one, but I'm being careful."

"Here we are," bringing the plates and napkins to the table. She handed Robert his beer and sat next to her son, handing him his soda. "I'm sorry about the lasagna, but I know you like pizza also," Claire said with a smile on her face.

Taking the first bite, Randall said, "Oh man, this is so good. I haven't had a good pizza in years, and you ordered from my favorite pizza place. Old John's has the best pizza in town, but they don't deliver. How did you get it?" He turned, giving his mother a messy kiss on her cheek. She laughed and wiped it off. She swatted his arm for him to stop.

"I told JJ that you were home, and he offered to deliver it for me. Old John is still around and checks on things now that JJ runs the business," his mother said.

Randall ate the last piece. While he was eating, his parents cleaned up the box and empty cans. They chose a movie to finish off the evening. When the movie was over, Randall said he was going to bed.

It had been a long, tiring day. He thanked his parents for dinner and headed up the steps. Half way up, he stopped, remembering that his bag was still in the car.

He turned to hobble back down when his dad came around the corner carrying his duffel. He walked it up and handed it to his son. Randall nodded and continued up the stairs. He didn't know when his dad went out to his car, but he was thankful he didn't have to make the trip. His leg had started to bother him. He needed to take his pain medication. His mother had told him that his room was to the right. He got inside and sat on the bed, rubbing his wounded leg. He noticed a bottle of water on the nightstand and gave thanks to his mother's thoughtfulness. He decided to take all his night pills and crawl into bed. He'd shower in the morning. He fell asleep to the murmurs of his parent downstairs.

Hours later, Claire watched as Robert drove off. She closed and locked the door. She placed her forehead on the door. What was she getting herself into? Yes, she missed her husband, but she's made a life for herself. Will he be willing to stay in one place? He said he retired from the Marines, but she knew, once a Marine always Marine. Well, she'd take it one day at a time. She still loved him and wanted to give it her best shot. She turned off the lights and went upstairs. She thought she'd check on Randall to see if he needed anything. She tapped on the door in case her son fell asleep. When he didn't answer, she couldn't resist a peek. It had been so long since her son was home. She opened the door a little ways, and what she saw terrified her. He twisted and turned in bed with a contorted expression of pain on his face.

Should she try to wake him? She knew he had pride and wouldn't want to trouble her, so she decided against it. Claire couldn't watch anymore. She backed out of his room and closed the door. She went to her room and cried herself to sleep.

Chapter 5

The creepy caller knew Rachael wouldn't ignore him now. She belonged to him. He thought he might have gone too far in destroying her studio, because now she left. She got into another lady's car, and he followed them. She must be staying there until her place got fixed. He sat in his car and watched. He needed to stick close, but he'd have to change positions. He didn't want anyone to get suspicious and call the cops. He needed to protect Rachael. He sent he another message letting her know he watched over her.

Melissa drove Rachael to her house, took her inside, and sat her down on the couch. Rachael moved in automation, not thinking. Shock took over her body. How could somebody do this? The studio was her home. Someone violated her space and smashed her whole life to smithereens. Melissa's voice penetrated the shock, as she ran her hand up and down her back in a soothing gesture.

"You can stay here until you find another workplace. There's plenty of room. Tomorrow, we'll go out and get you some stuff. I know you need clothes and a new computer." She spoke like she would a child, trying to get Rachael to relax.

Shaking her head, Rachael replied, "I don't want to be any trouble. I can stay at a hotel."

"No, please stay here, at least for tonight. We'll talk about what to do tomorrow. Let me show you to the guest room, so you can relax. Are you hungry? I can fix us some lunch." Rachael knew Melissa was handling her with kid gloves.

"No thank you. I'm not hungry. I think I'll just lie down for a little bit and relax. I know I need to work, but it can wait until tomorrow."

"Thank you, Melissa. You're the best friend anyone could ever have," giving her friend a hug. Rachael meant it to. She was ready to fall apart, but her friend's kind and supportive nature calmed her nerves. Rachael didn't know what she would have done if Melissa hadn't come for her. Seeing her beautiful apartment in such chaos caused her thoughts to scramble.

Melissa showed her to her room and where to find the towels, if she wanted to take a shower. She told Rachel she'd find an outfit for her to wear. The beast that broke into her place had shredded all her clothes along with smashing everything else. Someone truly didn't like her.

Later that afternoon, Rachael came out into the living room and found Melissa working on her computer. Not wanting to bother her, she went into the kitchen to get something to drink. She opened the refrigerator, got a bottle of water, and scooped some grapes from the dish.

Sitting down at the breakfast bar, she grabbed the notebook by the phone and a pencil. She listed all the things she had to get tomorrow. She needed to get a computer, so she could finish her manuscript. She remembered to take her wallet with her when she left her place. She still had some of the advance from her book that she could afford a decent computer to work with. There were some good thrift stores in the area, allowing her to get some clothes without spending too much. Thinking of anything else she absolutely needed, she noticed her car keys on the counter. The police must have driven it over for her. She was glad, because she didn't think she could go back to the building anytime soon.

Rachael thought about her living situation. She could stay in a hotel until she found something, but that would cut into her available cash. Besides, she'd had enough of the hotel life, between the tour and her attempted escape from her nightmarish calls. Maybe she'd accept Melissa's kind offer and stay with her for a short period of time.

She also decided to call her cell phone company and get her number changed. She didn't want to get anymore creepy calls. She'd turned her phone off when she went upstairs. She turned it on to call her carrier. Just as she was about to make the call, her phone chirped with an incoming message. She opened the message and immediately dropped her phone. It slid across the tile floor.

On the screen was a picture of the front of Melissa's house with a message saying, "I know where you are. You can't hide from me."

The sicko must've been watching when she left her building and then followed them. She called out to her friend, who came running into the kitchen and saw the phone on the floor. Melissa picked it up and stared at the message. About to delete it, Rachael stopped her saying, "We need to show the police this message. Maybe it will help them find this guy."

"You're right. I'll call the officer now." She went to her phone and dialed the number given to Rachael. After talking to the officer, there was a short pause before Melissa began speaking again. Rachael noticed a friendlier tone in her friend's voice. Melissa hung up and told Rachael that her case was assigned to Detective Tom Malone. She explained to her how she knew Tom and assured her that he was good at his job.

A short time later, a knock on the door startled Rachael. With Melissa busy in the kitchen, she went to the door and asked, "Who is it?"

"Detective Malone, ma'am," came the deep reply.

She cracked the door and asked, "Can I see some identification." The detective showed his badge, and Melissa confirmed from the kitchen doorframe that it was Tom. Rachael opened the door wide so he could step inside. Tom was about six feet and well built. One observation of him, one could tell he meant business. Her friend came in from the kitchen and gave Tom a hug, thanking him for coming. They all ambled into the living room and sat down.

"I peeked around outside and saw nothing unusual. I also checked the cars with clear sight of the house. There was nobody just sitting there. I'm guessing he's gone, but I'll have a car patrol around here every couple of hours to keep a check on thing. If you see or hear anything, let them know. Please, may I see the message he sent?" Tom asked in a calming voice.

Rachael brought up the message and handed her phone to him.

Malone got up and checked out the front window to see where the picture might've been taken. "There is no car across the street, so he must have moved," informed Tom.

"Do you have any idea who this guy is?" he asked Rachael, as handed back her phone.

"No. All this started a couple of weeks ago, right before my book tour I did to promote my latest book. I don't know why this guy is fixated on me. I don't remember doing anything to anyone, to draw this guy's attention."

"While searching your apartment for evidence, our CSU discovered a hidden camera across the hall from your door and one inside, facing the door. He was able to keep tabs on when you arrived and left. They didn't find any others, indicating he wasn't watching everything you did," declared Tom.

"Well, thank goodness for small favors," Rachael muttered.

He said to Rachael, "I have to go, but please call if anything else happens." Turning to Melissa, he said, "I think I'll take a rain check on that dinner tonight. You're needed here, and I've some paper work to finish."

"Okay, sounds great. Thanks for understanding." She followed him to the door and kissed him goodbye.

"I didn't mean to ruin your evening, Melissa. You should go out. I'll be fine."

"No, it's not a problem. Tom knows that you shouldn't be alone tonight. We'll chat later and make new plans. We've only been on a couple of dates, nothing serious. He's a great guy. Now, no more fuss about it. Come in the kitchen and help me with dinner. We'll watch some TV and make it an early night," she said. "We get to go shopping tomorrow," she squealed.

Rachael followed, shaking her head. Melissa's easygoing attitude was infectious.

Chapter 6

Randall's mother drove him crazy just after one morning. She kept asking if she could get him anything, acting like he was an invalid. That was why he needed his own space. Going further, she insisted he should find a good woman and settle down. The quicker he called Tom about using his parent's cabin, the better. He dialed the number and waited for an answer.

"Randall, great to hear from you buddy," exclaimed the voice on the phone. "Hey man, I heard about the accident. How are you?" Tom asked in a more somber tone.

"I've been better," Randall answered. "I was wondering if your family still had that cabin on the lake. I need any place quiet, away from my mom. Being discharged has left me floundering." Tom had been a close friend in school and it felt like the years slipped away hearing his voice again. He felt he could open up to him. "My leg aches, and at any loud sounds, I dive for cover. Solitude and peacefulness are requirements for my healing."

"Mom and Dad signed the cabin over to me, and it's available. It has exactly what you asked for. How about meeting for dinner tonight, and I'll give you the keys. We can catch up on what's been going on in our lives."

They agreed on a time, and they chose to go the Old John's pizza, where they hung out in high school.

Around noon, Randall's dad picked him up to find a vehicle since he was here to stay. At 7:00 p.m., Randall stepped out of his shiny new truck, as his friend parked next to him. They hugged and slapped each other's back, Tom's a little harder. "Good to see you buddy!" exclaimed Tom.

"Take it easy there," stammered Randall. "Good to see you, too."

"Hope you're hungry, because I sure am. I skipped lunch today. The same thing happens whenever I get a new case. I dive in and forget everything else." His stomach grumbled to prove his point.

"That's right. You're a detective now. My parents were trying to catch me up on some of the people I used to know. I am starving. My folks had pizza delivered last night, from none other than Old John's." He spread his arms toward the restaurant.

"They don't deliver. How did you manage that?"

"JJ brought it to help my mom out. I could eat Old John's pizzas seven days a week. Yummo!" he howled.

They sauntered into the restaurant and sat in the first available booth. The aromas in the place made Randall's mouth water. Randall notice that Tom observed his limp but didn't comment, thankfully.

Old John himself came over to take their order. When he got to the table, he said, "I remember two strapping boys that used to come in here all the time a few years back. It's good to see you both." He extended his hand out to Randall and they shook. "Thank you for your service. Sorry to hear about the accident. Glad you made it home though. Your pizza is on the house," John announced. Tom ordered the house special and two beers. Randall changed his to a soda, so Tom ordered two. John left to personally make their pizza.

"You could've had a beer. I'm on some meds, and I don't know how they would interact with alcohol," Randall explained.

"No problem. I might have to go back to work later anyway. So, how's it like being back home?"

"To tell you the truth, I don't like it. Don't get me wrong. It's not that I'm unhappy to see Mom and Dad again, but I want peace and quiet to come to terms with everything: the accident, the rehab, and the discharge. What do I do from here? When the Marines discharged me, I was devastated. Being a part of the unit was my whole life," he explained the best he could.

"Mom means well, but she wants to do everything for me. She acts like I'm some fragile individual that will fall apart. I have problems and she saw them first hand last night. I think it scared her. I have to work through this on my own. She's not happy I'm leaving, but it's the right thing for me."

"Wait a minute, back up. Did you say your dad was home?" exclaimed Tom.

Nodding, Randall stated, "Yes, I did. He retired. He and Mom want to try to get back together. I hope the best for them. However, being underfoot, she turns her focus on me, not on Dad. That's why the cabin will be a great escape."

"Well, here's the key, no strings attached. However, I do have a favor to ask. You can decline or tell me to bug off," he chuckled. "I have this case where a real psycho is stalking this pretty woman. At first, anonymous texts that progressed to phone calls and bouquets of flowers, then it escalated to breaking into her apartment and trashing it. When she left, he followed her to where she is staying with a female friend of mine. The cabin is large enough for two. You each would have your own space, if that is what you choose. She's a writer and will probably spend most of her time in her room. My favor is that you just keep a watch and make sure nothing happens. She doesn't even have to know. What do you say?" Tom asked, hoping Randall's time in the service would trigger his protectiveness.

"I don't know," he hedged, "peace and quiet, remember. I wasn't planning on company that may or may not bring trouble."

"Like I said, you might not even see her or know that she's there. She may go outside to hike around the lake, or take the canoe out. I'm sure she won't disturb you," reiterated Tom.

"Are you going to tell her I'll be there? If not, what am I to say? I don't want to scare her any more than she is," he hesitated.

"I'll let her know, just like I let you know, that the cabin is big enough for two, that there is plenty of space. You could come up with schedules for the common areas if you wanted.

"I won't tell her you'll be watching over her. I'm hoping she thinks going to the cabin will throw the man off her scent, and he'll get tired of harassing her," he explained. "That's my goal anyway."

"Okay buddy, I'll do it. Thanks for the use of the cabin. Hopefully, everything stays peaceful, and I can concentrate on my future. The walking will help strengthen my leg."

The pizza came and further talk of the cabin was suspended. Randall talked a little about the accident, because he knew Tom was curious. He didn't go into great detail, because some of the operation was still classified. Then they moved on to more pleasant things, like Tom and his female friend, Melissa. He could tell Tom liked this woman a lot by the smile on his face. She sounded like she'd brighten up Tom's Day after working some bad cases. The guys ate their fill, enjoying every bite. There were a few pieces left, so they asked for a takeout box. Tom told him to take it with him to the cabin. Randall packed his truck earlier so he could head out after dinner, much to him mother's dismay.

They strolled out to the parking lot and shook hands. "Thanks again for the use of the cabin. By-the-way, what is the name of woman coming to the cabin?"

"Her name is Rachael Simmons. She's a new author. The place that was destroyed served as her writing cave. You both will have access to my state-of-the-art computer system. Here's my password to login. Enjoy my friend."

"I'll keep a watch out and contact you if there is any trouble." With a final wave, they both got in their vehicles and drove away.

Tom was relieved his friend would keep a protective watch on Rachael. He didn't think there would be trouble, but having an experienced man on the job was helpful. Reviewing her file earlier, he knew Randall would be the right man. About 10:00 p.m., he called Melissa for their evening chat. "Sorry it is so late, babe. I had dinner with an old high school pal and came up with a plan for your friend." He explained what he discussed with Randall, and she liked the idea. Getting her friend out of the crosshairs of the psycho was great thinking.

She told him she would tell Rachael in the morning about sharing the cabin but didn't see any problems that would cause her to decline. They both agreed not to tell her about Randall watching out for any trouble. That would make her balk at the idea. The whole purpose was to get out the stalker's sight.

"I'll drop the keys and directions off first thing in the morning." They talked a little longer and then said their goodbyes.

Chapter 7

The stalker had to get Rachael alone. Maybe if he called, pretending to be the police, telling her a suspect was in custody and needed her to come to the station and identify him. No, that won't work because she'll bring her friend. There might be a chance she would recognize his voice. He needed her by herself. He could call and threaten to harm her friend if she didn't come out to the backyard by herself. He saw a gate to the back when checking for a way in. He'd call now before they went anywhere. She won't expect it to be him, because he knew she changed her number. It didn't take long for him to get the new one.

Early the next morning, Rachael came into the kitchen to make coffee. As she was measuring it out, her phone buzzed. The ID read the same: Unknown, "How can this be!" exclaimed Rachael, just as Melissa was coming into the kitchen, yawning.

"What's up?" she asked.

In response, Rachael slid her phone down the center island to her friend. When she saw the missed call and the ID, she asked, "Didn't you change your number? Maybe it's not him. There's a message, let's see." She pulled up the voicemail and put it on speaker. A grating voice said, "You thought you could get away from me by changing your number. I know every move you make, even before you do. You can never get rid of me."

The message continued, but Melissa clicked the end button and plunked down in the bar stool at the counter. "Well, I do have a place where you can go that I don't believe this reprobate could ever find you. Tom has a cabin, with a very nice computer system, I might add.

"He has offered to let you use both the cabin and computer giving you the opportunity to work on your book. It's on a lake which has a two mile path around, so you can exercise. It also has a canoe, if you feel adventurous."

"That sounds perfect! When can I go?" Getting away from this creep sounded too good to pass up. Melissa gave her a piece of paper with directions, Tom's phone number, and the keys he dropped off before he went to work.

"You can be on your way anytime. We can hit some thrift stores this morning for some clothes, have lunch, and then you can head off."

"That sounds great. Let's have some coffee and then get started on our day." Rachael felt a heaviness lifted off her.

"I do need to tell you one thing first. Tom is letting an old high school friend use the second bedroom. He's recuperating from some trauma he went through and needed a quiet place. The cabin is huge. There is plenty of room for two without seeing each other. You can work out the details of the living area and kitchen. I'm sure he'll spend most of his time in his room, wanting solitude. To finish your book, you will also," she explained.

"It still sounds too good to pass up. I'm sure we can work out some arrangements. Thanks, Melissa," she proclaimed.

"Don't thank me. It's Tom's cabin. He thinks you'll be safe there, and this sick guy will eventually give up," she responded.

After their coffee and light breakfast, they took both cars, so Rachael could leave when they were through. They visited five thrift stores, and Rachael decided she had enough clothes to last her for months. She found a suitcase to carry the purchases. They went into a garden restaurant next to the last thrift shop and ordered salads and water. Waiting for the order, Rachael observed a man glaring at her from across the garden. She shivered from the stare. She didn't know this man, but he seemed vaguely familiar. Why was he looking at her like that? Just as she was going to tell Melissa, he stomped off. Rachael shook it off, thinking she must have been mistaken. Their order came, and she put the man out of her mind. As they were walking to their cars, Rachael felt someone watching her. She checked around but found no one paying attention to her.

That episode in the restaurant must have frightened her more than she thought. When they got to their cars, Melissa gave her a hug, and also a cell phone she bought along their excursions. Melissa told her that it could not be traced back to her, and she was the only one with the number. Melissa explained she wanted Rachael to have some way to reach her if there was trouble. She also suggested switching cars with her. That way, if someone was following or there was some kind of tracker on Rachael's car, they wouldn't find her. They hugged one last time and went their separate ways.

Rachael, still concerned with those feelings of being watched, drove around and cut through alleys before heading on to the cabin. Tom had given very good directions. Every few moments, she would check the rear view mirror to see if anyone was following. She had driven sixty miles when the turn off for the lake came into view. Again, she checked all mirrors, and she even drove past the road to a tiny market, just to be sure. She bought a few things to eat. She didn't know what was at the cabin, so she wanted to be prepared, just in case.

When she left the mini market, she didn't feel any sensation of being watched, so she drove back to the turnoff. Two miles down the road, she saw the drive for the cabin. When she arrived, a truck was already parked. She hoped it belonged to Tom's friend. As she put the car in park, trying not to block the truck, a very handsome stranger came out the door. He came to the car and opened the door for her. "Are you Tom's friend? I hope I'm not intruding. Melissa said there was room for two. I'll try to stay out of your way," she rambled.

"My name is Randall Lewis. I just got off the phone with Tom, and he let me know that they'd told you I'd be here. I hope sharing isn't a going to be a problem. The cabin is indeed big enough for the both of us, and we can work out any difficulties on the common areas. I came for some peace and quiet, so I'll be spending most of my time in my room and maybe canoeing," he clarified.

He was easy on the eyes, and there were worse things than sharing a cabin with such a gorgeous man. She would be staying in her room, most of the time, working. She agreed there were no problems.

He helped carry in the groceries she picked up, and Rachael carried her bag and purse. "By the way, my name is Rachael Simmons."

"Hello, Rachael." Randall gave her a cheerful smile.

Rachael was amazed at the size of the cabin, and the layout was perfect. The two bedrooms were on each side with a huge kitchen and large living area in the middle. The living area had a couch with a coffee table, a couple of chairs and a table by the window, and a state of the art entertainment package. Each bedroom had its own door that led outside, so each of them could come and go without bothering the other. It seemed that Randall had picked the bedroom on the right, so she took her stuff in the room on the left. It had a queen size bed with a beautiful quilt on it, a pale yellow dresser that matched the quilt, pale yellow sheer curtains on the windows, and a desk with an awesome computer system on it. Tom must really like his electronic gadgets, she thought to herself. Each bedroom had its own bath. After putting her stuff away, she wandered back into the living area. Randall was in the kitchen fixing something that smelled awfully enticing.

"It smells awesome in here. What are you cooking?"

"I caught some fish in the lake. Tom said it was okay to eat anything I caught. I'm using the indoor grill to grill them and some vegetables. Are you hungry?" he asked, being very hospitable.

"I'm hungry, but I don't want to impose," she replied, having only picked at her lunch.

"Nonsense, I made enough for two, so you wouldn't be imposing. I figured you might be hungry after your drive out here. If you set the table on the patio, we can have a view of the lake as we eat."

As the paper plates and plastic utensils were on the counter, she picked them up and went out the slider to a big patio. She set up the table and checked around the back of the cabin. There was a path that led to a dock. It also led to the trail around the lake. The shrubbery blocked most of lake from the cabin. A big shed was close to the dock where the canoe must be. It was a beautiful spot on the lake. She stepped back into the kitchen to see if she could help. "Everything's ready. If you could get a couple bottles of water out of the refrigerator, I'll bring the rest out."

Rachael got the water and followed him out to the table. They both sat and served themselves.

Along with the fish, he grilled some squash, zucchini, and peppers, and made a fruit salad. The food tasted as good as it smelled. As they were eating, she asked, "So, what do you do?"

Randall was hoping not to get into this predicament of having to tell Rachael about himself, but it would be rude to ignore the question. He just said he was between jobs and left it at that. "Tom tells me you are a writer, what kind of books?"

She answered, "Fiction suspense books. I've only written one, and the other is due to my agent by the end of month. I'll be working on that so you won't be seeing much of me for the next few days. I thought I was done, but rereading it, there are a few places I need to clean up. My studio was trashed, so Tom and Melissa thought the cabin would be an ideal place to work."

"What happened to your place?" he inquired, even though Tom had told him about the break in.

"Some nut job broke in and wreaked my apartment, broke my laptop, smashing my hard drive. Luckily, I copied my work onto a thumb drive before I left. The room screamed 'disaster zone,'" she fumed.

"Do you know who did it?" he asked, wanting to know if she knew the person.

"No, but he'd been calling me but said nothing, just heavy breathing. When I didn't answer the phone, he'd be angry the next time I forgot to check the ID and answered. He placed a camera in the hall and one in my workplace, both focused on the door. So whenever I came or left, I'd get the calls. He even followed me over to Melissa's place and texted a picture of the front of the house. He wanted to let me know I couldn't get away from him," she stammered.

"This guy sounds certifiable!" he hissed.

"I'm sorry, I didn't mean to pour this out to you. You're a complete stranger. Why should you care if I have a stalker?

"Since we're finished eating and you cooked, I'll clean up and spend the evening working on my revisions." She gathered the dishes to toss in the garbage and headed inside to clean the kitchen. Before entering the cabin, Rachael said, "We could make an arrangement. You're such a good cook, you could continue in that capacity. I'll clean, and we'll split the groceries. How does that sound?"

"That sounds okay with me. If you ever want to try your hand at cooking, we'll just switch duties. Might as well cook for two as long as we're cooking," he answered.

While Rachael cleaned the cooking dishes, she watched Randall stroll down to the dock through the window. She, again, noticed the limp and wondered what had happened. He didn't talk about any accident. Was it an old injury or did it recently happen? He was tall, about six inches over her five foot nine inch height. His body was lean. Maybe a little too thin, but Tom did say he just got out of the hospital. Randall had chestnut brown hair, with red highlights that showed when the sun's rays shined on his head. He had the prettiest blue eyes. One could stare into them and feel peace and tranquility. She gave herself a shake. She wasn't here to dally. She had a book to finish. She wiped her hands and headed to her room.

Chapter 8

Where did she go? The stalker followed her car back to the lady's house, but Rachael wasn't the woman who exited the car. They must have switched. He tried calling her, but it went straight to voice mail, like it has been turned off. She was mistaken if she thought she can get away from him. He'd find her. He slammed the car in drive and peeled off down the road. He had to find her. He'd check deed records tomorrow to see if she had any other properties. She belonged to him, and he wanted her back where he could see her.

Rachael heard Randall come in and lock up. It was close to ten o'clock. She decided to break for the night and start fresh in the morning. The ending scene was not coming together like she had hoped. A few laps around the lake and the fresh air will clear her head and, hopefully, spark her creativity. She saved her work and put the thumb drive in her bag. She knew in case of an emergency, she would always pick up her bag. She took a nice hot shower to relax her, after hours sitting at the computer, and crawled in a very comfortable bed, turning out the light. She heard Randall in the shower and fantasies of joining him took over. She needed to start thinking of something else to get her mind off the sexy body in the shower. They both came for the peace and quiet, not a vacation romance.

A couple of hours of the house being silent, Rachael heard this horrendous scream. She sat upright in bed and wondered what it could be. It didn't sound like any animal she'd ever heard, but she never spent much time in the country. As soon as her heart stopped pounding, the terrible noise rang out again. This time, she went to investigate. She looked out her patio door and couldn't see anything outside. She'd check to see if Randall heard it.

Tiptoeing to her door, she silently pulled it open. Crossing through the living room, she heard it again. The sound came from his room.

He cried out as though in agony. Maybe some wild creature broke through his patio door. He shrieked with such torment, she couldn't let it go. She tapped on his door and received no response. Opening the door, she observed him twisting and turning in his bed. He must be having a gruesome nightmare, and she thought she should wake him up. Easing over to the bed, Rachael called his name. Still, no response. She stepped closer to shake his shoulder, repeating his name. His arms were moving so fast, his right fist connected with her eye. He was screaming, "Get away from me. I have to save my team. I have to get them out of the fire. Get away!"

Rachael's right side of her face throbbed, but the greater need was to get him settled before he did damage to his leg. She tried again, "Randall, wake up. You're having a nightmare." He started to calm down. She repeated the words in a low, calm voice until he rested in peace in his bed. Once stable, she left the room. Rachael didn't want him to see that he hit her. He did not strike her on purpose but would feel awful for the act. Stopping in the kitchen, she grabbed an ice pack and took it to her room. Placing it on the sore spot, she hoped the swelling would go down. Rachael would have to come up with a plausible story in case he noticed the bruising.

The next morning, she awakened at 6:00 a.m., did some stretches, and headed out her patio door. Avoiding Randall, she trekked around the back of the house and found the trail. The eye hurt and a glance in the mirror confirmed she couldn't hide it from him. She decided her day would be spent in her room. Hiking around the lake, her mind focused on the revisions that needed to be done. One more week until her agent was expecting her manuscript. Taking some deep breaths, she picked up her speed to let the exercise release her creative flow.

Finishing the second lap, she quickened her pace toward her side of the cabin. The slider from the main section opened and Randall stepped out. She stopped in her tracks, gazing at the perfect male body in shorts and a tank top, leaving little to the imagination. Forgetting to shield the bruising, she said, "Good morning. Are you going for a walk?"

Randall stared at her slim body covered in yoga pants and tank top. His body responded to the natural beauty, but something was off. He took another view of her face, and asked, "What happened to the side of your head?"

"Oh, when I was opening a cabinet, my eye got in the way. It looks worse than it feels," she lied.

"You're going to have a good shiner. I'm actually going for a run. The leg needs a good work out. I'll run as long as I can, then slow the pace down," he asserted.

"Well, be careful," she warned. "There are some bare roots and dips in the path. Tripping on them could make your leg worse. A rut appears on this side of the bridge that could twist an ankle if you step wrong. Maybe walk the first lap and see how it goes," suggested Rachael.

"We'll see." She understood that to mean he wouldn't heed her advice.

Randall trekked down the path and started to jog. Typical male, had to do things his way. Shaking her head, she traipsed into her room and set up her coffee pot. A habit ingrained in her to take it everywhere because most hotel coffee sucks. The pot being in her room meant less interaction with her roommate. Since he was out of the cabin, she went to the kitchen to grab some fruit and a power bar.

By the time she returned, the coffee finished brewing. She poured herself a mug, added some cream, and put the lid on tight. No open drinks around the computer. One time, her coffee spilt onto her computer. What a disaster! From then on, she used an insulated mug with a lid. Sitting at the computer, she glanced out the window as the object of her night fantasies passed by. "I guess he made the loop okay," she said to herself. Once the computer booted up, she retrieved and inserted her thumb drive. As the words came on the screen, she scrolled to the part last worked on. Her fingers hovered over the keyboard as she checked outside to make sure Randall made it back. Not concentrating on the story, she gave up. Taking her coffee to the back patio, Rachael waited for Randall's return.

A half hour went by and still no Randall. Maybe he took a rest break. She needed to get him off her mind and get back to her revisions.

Back in front of her computer, she glanced out the window one last time and saw him limping badly. Undecided whether she should go help, she knew him to be a proud man and didn't want to show weakness. On the other hand, his grimace and uneven gait meant he had to be in a lot of pain. She decided to go help him, expecting him to refuse. He gladly accepted the assistance and put his arm around her shoulder. It eased some weight off his sore leg.

"I guess I should have listened to you. I made it one time around and thought I could make a second lap. I hit a bare root, followed by stepping in a dip with my bad leg. It gave out. Being more than half way around, I hobbled the rest of the way. My leg hurts like hell." The agony on his face told the story.

She helped him into the cabin to the couch, and Randall all but fell on it. "Where are your pain pills?" She growled at him. Men with their stupid pride. If he had only listened to her.

"They're the capsules in the medicine cabinet," he responded with a grimace.

Rachael found the pills and filled a glass with water. She tossed the bottle on his lap and held the glass until he was ready. With an unhappy face, she joined him on the sofa. He took the pills, reclined back, and let out a big sigh.

"Sorry I didn't listen to you. I felt like I could make two laps, since the first one caused no problems. I'll take it easy from now on. My leg won't heal in one day," he remarked. Rachael heard the frustration in his voice.

"No, it won't. Maybe you should take tomorrow off from strenuous leg exercises. You'll only aggravate it." She started rubbing the area around his scars, and he let out another heavy sigh. He enjoyed her massage, even though it was stimulating something else on his body.

Randall let himself relax and fell asleep. Rachael let him be. Now that he was back, she concentrated on her work, and the revision went easier. She figured out the problem that was stumping her. Her stomach growled indicating it was time to break for lunch. Going out to the main area, she noticed Randall had stretched out on the couch, but awake.

"I'm going to fix a sandwich. Would you like me to make you one?"

"That would be great. Thank you." He hobbled to the counter and sat on the bar stool. Bringing the fixings and two bottle of waters, they made their own sandwiches and ate in silence.

"Go rest and I'll clean up."

He didn't argue. He limped back to the couch. "I've a question to ask you. What really happened to your eye?" He didn't believe for one second that a cabinet door hit created the swelling and bruising on her face.

She thought about sticking to her story, but something in his voice changed her mind. She gazed at him and saw the concern. "You were having a nightmare and I tried to wake you up. Your swinging arms caught me unaware. You fist connected with my eye."

"Oh, damn. I'm really sorry I hit you!" he exclaimed.

"You were asleep. You didn't know what you were doing. Let's forget it. It's not hurting as much now. In a day or two, it'll hardly be noticeable."

"Have you seen it lately? The bruising will take more than a couple of days." It'll be a constant reminder how much he hurt her, however, unintentionally.

Chapter 9

When Rachael left room, Randall called Tom.

"Hello buddy. How's it going at the cabin?"

"Not great. I socked Rachael during one of my nightmares," he grunted. "I didn't do it on purpose. She tried to wake me up. Apparently, I was swinging my arms around and my fist wacked her in the eye. I'm afraid of hurting her more. Maybe this wasn't such a good idea. I don't know if I move around in my nightmares, considering she said I called out about saving my team. What if I go into her room and cause more damage. You should get someone else to watch her, and I'll find another quiet place."

Tom said. "I don't think you'll hurt her. She's aware you might attack, so she'll be more cautious. Believe me, you are the best man to protect her. Shit happens. I don't know to what extent this stalker will go. He could figure out where she went, though I don't know how. I trust you to be there for her."

"Okay. If you're sure, I'll stay," he responded.

After the call, Randall went into his room and worked on weights to build upper body strength. Tom's cabin included a weight bench and dumbbells. When he exhausted himself, he took a shower. The hot water streaming on his leg eased the muscle tension. Shutting off the water, he dried off and wrapped a towel around his waist. Laying down on the bed, he drifted off for a short nap.

Upon waking, he dressed in some jeans and a t-shirt and ambled, without much trouble, to the kitchen to start dinner.

Chapter 10

Rachael didn't know what time it was, but something started smelling delicious. Wrapping up for the day, she saved her work, printed out her revisions, and shut the computer down. Tonight, she'd relax and read a book. Her final scene broke through and she needed another day to finish it.

Stepping out of her room, her phone rang. She answered the call, knowing her friend was the only one with the new number. Melissa stated, "Don't freak out, but someone broke into my house. Nothing serious, things were moved around as though the perpetrator searched for something. Unfortunately, your number was on a folded piece of paper on the cork board, and now it's missing. I'm sorry. Your calls may start again. However, he doesn't know where to find you."

"Thanks for the heads up. Are there any leads to the psycho's identity? Did they get any fingerprints?" she probed.

"No, they're still working on it. Since he broke into my home, Tom's boss added more officers to the case. They want him caught before he hurts somebody." They talked a few more minutes.

Entering the kitchen area, Randall observed her pinched face and asked, "What's up? You look as though someone kicked your dog."

She conveyed what Melissa told her. "My phone will probably start ringing nonstop. Melissa purchased a prepaid phone for my use. I left mine with her."

"Best of intentions." Changing the subject, he added, "I hope you're hungry. I fixed burgers and fries."

"Sounds awesome. How's the leg? I hope you are resting it," she teased.

"You sound like my mother. Yes, staying off it all afternoon relieved the pain. The massage helped," he winked. "I'll take your advice and skip my run tomorrow. I thought of canoeing for exercise. Would you like to go?"

"I wish I could, but I'm on deadline. This whole stalker thing has put me behind schedule. I believe my revisions will be complete tomorrow. After that, I'm free to have a little fun."

"Can I read it when you're done?"

"I usually don't let anyone read it until my publisher is set to go on it, but I can't see where it would hurt. I'd love your input. Do you like suspense books?"

"It depends. If it catches my attention quickly, I'll continue. Otherwise, I give up," shrugging his shoulders.

After dinner, they enjoyed a spectacular sunset. Rachael cleared the table and scrubbed the inside grill. Randall stayed on the porch, resting his leg in the lounger. She brought out refreshments, a glass of wine for her and a bottle of water for him. They appreciated the serenity of the night.

Around midnight, they called it a night. He caught her arm, and said, "It's strange how comfortable I'm with you. I don't feel panicky like I do around others. Thank you for your help this afternoon. I'll heed your advice from now on. Good night."

Rachael told him good night and went to her room. She felt the same way. She felt more relaxed around him. Her arm still tingled where he touched her, and she wondered what it would feel like with his hands in different places. Shaking the thoughts out of her head, she got ready for bed and turned off the light. Her phone started ringing. She checked the id then turned it off, throwing it across the room. She snuggled down and sleep claimed her.

Chapter 11

Morning found Randall awake before the sun rose. Closing his eyes, he imagined something happening to Rachael on her travel around the lake and no way to get to her. His frustration with his gimpy leg kept him awake. To ease his tension, he decided to get up and join her for a lap. After all, he was there to protect her.

He waited on the porch, ready to go, when Rachael rounded the cabin. She hadn't seen him yet, and started her stretching. He shamelessly watched as her yoga pants became tight on her ass when she bent over. He thought he died and gone to heaven. He would love to have her bend over so he could slide inside her. He hardened thinking about it. He turned away to control his rising erection. He did some stretching of his own. When he was finished, she glanced at him with a raised eyebrow.

"My leg feels much better today. I thought I would try the trail with you if you don't mind. Just one lap. I promise not to slow you down. If I can't meet your pace, you go ahead. I'll take it easy."

"Sure. Exercising with someone would be better, just in case you do happen to fall."

They set off at a moderate pace. Picking up speed about half way around. He felt his leg start to ache, but he needed to push his tolerance a little. They completed the first lap, and Randall stayed at the cabin. He watch Rachael take off at a jog for her second lap. He stretched before sitting down to wait for her.

During the wait, he concluded he was paranoid. Just because the pursuer had her number didn't mean he could find her. Last night, he heard her phone and a thump.

She must have thrown the offending object across the room. They needed more groceries, so he went in to shower and head off to the grocery story. He left a note to let her know where he went.

At the market, he picked up another prepaid phone. He understood the stress the unwanted calls caused Rachael. Similar to his mother doing everything for him. Back at the cabin, he unloaded the groceries before heading to her closed door. He tapped lightly. When she opened it, he handed her the phone, explaining, "When I shopped, I picked it up. I thought you might need it."

"Thank you, that was really thoughtful," she replied with shimmering tears. "I shut off the other one and considered my options. I emailed my agent informing her of the problem. She responded that emailing would work until this guy was caught."

"You still need one. With the sound of your phone hitting the wall last night, I figured the calls started again. Keep the first one off. Actually, take the battery out. I don't know if it can be traced but better safe than sorry. I loaded one hundred minutes of prepaid time, and the phone already came with fifty minutes. That should last until you get a new phone."

"Thank you. How much do I owe you?" Rachael grabbed her purse.

"Nothing, I'm helping out a friend. Pay it forward sometime," he replied.

"Okay, I brewed some coffee, would you like a cup?"

"Sure. Then I'll leave you alone. I need to do some research on jobs, something a lame guy could do," he grumbled.

Rachael poured a cup of coffee, and said, "You can do anything you set your mind to. There are plenty of jobs out there. How about private security or private investigation? Don't beat yourself up because you had a minor setback with the leg. In time it'll strengthen. Maybe not fully, but if you're sensible with your rehab, the limp will be almost unnoticeable." Handing him the mug, she backed off holding her hands up as though to emphasize that was the last she would say. "Thanks again for the phone." She smiled.

"No problem, and thanks for the coffee." Randall returned the smile, lifting the cup.

He strolled off with the door closing behind him after a slight delay. He smiled again, thinking she probably checked him out like he did her earlier. He sat on the couch with his computer, propping his leg up. Rubbing his sore area a few times during his searches.

He got lost in researching private security, and time flew by. Around three o'clock his stomach grumbled. He had skipped breakfast, having only the coffee. He went into the kitchen to figure something out for lunch.

Her door opened and she asked, "Is there something for lunch or would you like to go to the deli? I have to mail a letter."

"The deli sounds good. Plus it'll get you out of the cabin for a break. I know you hike but it's not the same." He didn't want her to go to the market by herself.

At the deli, they ordered, and she excused herself. She heads over to the little counter that housed a small post office. Depositing her envelope, she returned to the table.

"I finished my manuscript and this is a little celebration."

"That's great. Would you like to go canoeing tomorrow?"

"That would be awesome."

Their order came and Randall took a big bite of his Italian sub. He moaned and said, "This is so good."

"My steak and cheese is scrumptious."

"I'll have to try it next time."

"Do you know if we can swim in the lake? I would like to get some upper body exercise. I don't have any weights."

"The day you arrived, I took the canoe out. I saw people swimming. So I guess the answer would be yes. I can asked Tom to verify if you would feel safer. There's some weights in my room, but they are probably heavier than you use."

"Are they dumbbells that the weights can be removed? If so, I could use the bar," she suggested.

"Yes, why didn't I think of that? After my morning workout, I'll remove the weights and leave the bar on the porch, so you can use it when you return. By the way, I investigated the jobs you suggested."

"Does it sound like something you would be interested in?" she inquired.

"I think so, yes. My dad did a lot of security in his time in the service. I'll get his opinion when I go back."

When they finished, Randall asked, "Would you mind driving back so I can call Tom and check in."

"Not a problem, I'm curious if they're making progress on finding this guy."

Tom answered, "Randall, you're on my list of things to do. Is anything happening up there?"

"The calls started again last night. We got a new phone. The other is turned off and battery removed. I don't know if he's smart enough to trace it or not, but we don't want to take any chances. Is there any news on your end?"

"No. This guy is like a ghost. No clues left in Melissa's house or Rachael's studio. I don't think he can trace Rachael to the cabin, but continue to keep a watch out. I'm sorry I don't have more."

"No problem. We'll keep our eyes and ears opened." He didn't want Rachael to know he was asked to protect her. "Hey Tom, what do you need to get a private investigation license?"

Tom told him the requirements and said he would text the number of a guy in the business. Randall could talk to him before making any decisions. Randall thanked him and ended the call.

"Any new news?"

He hated to disappoint her. He shook his head. Her shoulders drooped. Trying to cheer her up, he asked, "Are you going to write another book?"

"I have a contract for at least three books. I emailed my second one to my agent and overnighted a thumb drive as backup. What a relief to have completed in time. I don't like cutting it so close to the deadline. That scoundrel screwed up my schedule big time. I was interrupted so many times while trying to work in my studio, and I hardly got anything accomplished. I left for three days because of lack of concentration. I tried various spots and still didn't write a word. Before all the craziness, I had to take a break to do a book tour to promote the first book, but I'd allotted time for that in my schedule. I'm ecstatic that it is finished." She smiled and her whole face lit up. He had to remind himself, safety, from him and her shadow.

Back at the cabin, he asked, "Can I read the book now that it is done?"

"Okay, I've a printed copy in my room. I'll warn you now, it may not have enough action for you. After all, you were in the military. I bet you saw a lot of action." Rachael wished she could take back the words when she saw the pained expression. Then it was gone. Maybe she imagined it. She went into her room to get the printout and told him to choose a movie.

Randall picked a comedy, because laughter was good for the soul. It was hilarious. They both laughed so hard, tears streamed down their faces. With the late lunch, neither wanted dinner. They said good night and went to their respective rooms for an early night.

With little sleep the night before, exhaustion over took Randall's body. He stripped, took his medication, and crawled into bed. He would shower after his exercising in the morning. His leg ached, but sleep claimed him as soon as his head hit the pillow. His nightmare began, reliving the agony of seeing his men. Then it changed. The bad images were disappearing and turned good, really good. If all his nightmares ended like this, he could survive them. The dream was so real. He was getting aroused visualizing a sexy body instead of seeing all the gore of his previous nightmares. He imagined kissing lips that were soft as silk. Then his mouth started to roam over the face and down the neck. He heard a moan and thought it was him. He continued down and brought his hand to the most perfect breast he had ever encountered. He sucked on it through a silky teddy. He was so caught up in his dream.

His hand continued down her body and found her sweet spot. It was so damp. He couldn't resist putting his fingers in her and rubbed her nub with his thumb.

Randall removed his fingers and tore off the panties. He pushed inside her. She was tight, thank goodness she was so wet. He wasn't taking his time. It had been a long dry spell, and he was afraid this dream would end before he did. He kept thrusting inside her. He could feel her getting closer. One more time and she exploded. She tightened around him each time he entered into her, milking him and made him explode. He gave out a big moan and spilled his seed. This dream was fantastic. He hoped he had it again and again. He pulled out of her, rolled over, and continued to sleep.

Chapter 12

When Rachael went into her room, she wasn't ready for bed. She was pumped because the manuscript was done and sent to Gretchen. She leafed through a magazine she brought with her. She must have dozed because she was startled awake with a loud scream. Remembering the first night, she immediately went to Randall's room. He was having another nightmare. She didn't want to get too close to his swinging arms, but she wanted to wake him up. She went to the other side of the bed and shook him, saying, "Randall, wake up. You are having a bad dream. Come on, wake up." No response. He was still screaming. She could make out some names. They must have been the names of his teammates. She tried again. This time he rolled over and grabbed her, pulled her on the bed, and kissed her like she had never been kissed before.

She knew it was wrong to respond, because he didn't know who he was kissing. He wasn't aware he was still dreaming. It was very real to her. He was still sleeping and kissing her as if his life depended on it. Before she could think twice, she threw her arms around his neck and kissed him back. It had been ages for her, and it felt so good. She could indulge a little, even if he wouldn't remember anything in the morning.

He was doing wonderous things to her body that made her tingle all over. She should stop him, but she didn't want the feeling to end. She thought her moans would wake him, but they only spurred him on. Trying to keep quiet, she didn't want wake him. However, when his fingers entered her, she about exploded. Then he started rubbing her, and she felt an orgasm coming. Her hips moved with his fingers. She was getting closer, but he pulled his fingers out. She thought maybe he woke up.

She was afraid to open her eyes because of what he might think of her.

When she peeked, his was still unaware. She sighed in relief.

She noticed he was naked and his cock was hard. Did she want him in her? Could she really go that far? She wasn't a virgin, but he still didn't know what he was doing. She wondered how he would feel inside her. She felt it grow harder on her belly. What was the harm? He wouldn't remember. She kept telling herself that, even though she knew it was wrong.

When he tore her panties and pushed inside of her, all was lost. Her thoughts settled and felt alive for the first time in a long time. Her hips match his thrusts. It felt wonderful and she let herself go. Before she knew it, he released inside her with a loud moan. He pulled out of her, rolled over and continued to sleep.

She couldn't move for a few minutes. She'd had sex before, but nothing close to this. She heard him snore and knew he never woke up. She silently got out of bed and picked up her torn panties.

Back in her room, she went over the whole thing again. She couldn't believe he didn't wake up, but was glad he didn't. She usually was not into one-night stands, but this was different. Randall wasn't awake. He dreamt it, and her dreams came true. The experience was earth-shattering. How would she face him in the morning? How was she to act the same way toward him? He was just some guy, who happened to share a cabin with her. She'd follow his lead. If he didn't say anything, neither would she. She rolled over, went to sleep, and had the best dreams.

His calls went unanswered. He had to find Rachael because she might be in trouble. Their connection was gone. She's too far away, and he felt incomplete without her. He believed she was his other half. Where would she go? She didn't go back to her studio. He watched daily for any sign of her. She's not at her friend's place. At the restaurant he last saw her, one car disappeared out of town. What was out there for her to go to? When he found her, he would make her pay for making him worry. She wasn't safe if he could not protect her. She belonged to him. He'd break into friend's house again, turning the place upside down searching for any hints. There must be some clue around that would help him find his soul mate. He would not stop until they were together again. He didn't find anything when he checked the property deeds under her name or relatives.

She's alone, just like him. That's why they were supposed to be together. Waiting outside her friend's house, he saw her pulling out of the driveway. He'd wait a little, just to be sure. Once inside, he searched thoroughly. Her friend had to know where she went, and he was going to find out.

Chapter 13

A couple of days went by since that wonderful, horrible night. Rachael went on as if nothing happened, because that was how Randall handled it. He must not have recalled the incident. Mind blowing sex and he doesn't remember. "That's just great," Rachael thought to herself. At least there had been no more nightmares.

Each day, they walked one lap together at a moderate pace. Then he turned off to do his weight workout on the porch as she jogged the second lap. When she returned to the porch, the weights from the bar were removed, freeing it for her workout.

One day, she felt him watching her. She usually went into her room to stretch after exercising, but decided to give him a show. She hoped he'd make a move on her. Sleep eluded her with him so close. He hadn't had more nightmares, which was a good thing. However, not having the excuse of waking him up, she was unable to be close to him again. She wished for a repeat. The first move would have to come from her. A fling was not her thing, but with such a hot guy and all this peace and quiet, what was a girl supposed to do? She would plan a strategy. For now, she required a shower.

While getting dressed, something smelled delicious. She loved having a man who cooked. Her experience in the kitchen provided her with boiling water. She relied on takeout and leftovers. Rachael wondered to the main area, and asked, "What's cooking?"

"Vegetable omelets. I figured we go to the trouble of working out, we should eat healthy."

His dazzling smile caused shivers to shoot down her body.

The smile made his face twice as handsome, and he was already the most gorgeous man she knew.

Getting her thoughts back to breakfast, Rachael took the utensils to the patio table. On the lounge chair was the printed pages of her manuscript. She smiled seeing some of the pages were flipped over. Going back inside, she poured two cups of coffee and took them to the table. He followed, carrying the plates of food. They sat and dug into the food.

"OMG. I've never had an omelet taste this good. You have the magic touch when it comes to cooking!" she exclaimed, covering her mouth when she talked.

"That's not the only magic touch I have." He winked at her.

Was he flirting with her? She smiled, and responded, "Oh yeah. What other magic touches do you have?"

"Someday I just might show you," joked Randall.

She blushed, remembering all too well his magic touches.

"I started your book last night. It grabbed my attention." He gave her a thumbs up.

After cleanup, they relaxed on the loungers. Randall's phone rang. He excused himself and sauntered down the path to the dock.

Rachael watched his expression and knew something was wrong. She ambled his way to give him time to finish. When he lowered the phone, she asked, "Is something wrong?"

He didn't think it would be fair to keep this from her, so he told her to sit down. Sitting on the edge of the dock with their feet dangling, he started, "Tom explained your situation when I asked about using the cabin and that you'd be here. He asked me to keep a watch out. His call just now was telling me that someone ransacked Melissa's house." Sensing Rachael's unease, he placed his hand on her arm and quickly continue, "She didn't get physically attacked because she wasn't home. However, Melissa is pissed. She's staying with Tom until this is over. The intruder grabbed her address book.

"It contains all her contacts including this address. He expressed concern for your safety. Keep a watch out for anything out of the ordinary. We stick together, safety in numbers."

"I know first-hand how destructive this guy can be. I'm glad Melissa is safe. Why didn't you tell me Tom asked you to watch over me? You know what, forget I asked. I should leave, go to a hotel. Me not being here will assure you aren't in danger." She stood and turned to leave.

He grabbed her wrist, and said, "No, wait, please stay. Yes, at first, I kept watch as Tom asked, but I like you and want to help. The danger could be nothing. However, he has this address, so I would be in the crosshairs. You only endanger yourself more by leaving. Let me protect you. Please, stay," he pleaded.

Rachael sighed, "Okay." With her head hanging down, she trudged to her room. When she was upset, writing tended to calm her. She jotted down ideas that ran through her mind. Some melded together to use for her next book. The process distracted her from thoughts of the stalker for a short time. This guy had to be caught soon, so she could get her life back. She thought about Randall. Would he keep in touch or was this just a job for him? Putting her head back, she contemplated the future. Since that steamy night, sleep eluded her.

Chapter 14

Meanwhile, Randall received another call. "Hi Mom, how are things going?"

"Fine dear. I was wondering about you. Have you been resting your leg? Have you decided what to do? When are you coming home? I thought I would see you more than just a day. I miss you."

"I miss you too, Mom," he responded. He'd spend more time with her when Rachael was safe. "How are you and Dad doing?" he asked, dodging her other questions.

"Well, it's a work in progress. Some days good, some not so much. It's been a long time since I had anyone personally in my life and the same for your father. I want our relationship to be repaired, so I'll keep plugging along," she vowed. They chatted for a bit before hanging up.

No sooner did he set the phone down, Tom called again. "Bad news, buddy," he stated ominously. "Some guy visited Melissa's mother. When she refused to answer any of his questions, he pushed her into the house and beat her. She's in the hospital with a broken jaw, a broken right arm, and a lot of cuts and bruises."

"How's Melissa holding up?" he inquired, knowing if it was his mother, he'd be stark raving mad.

"Melissa is so angry, she's spitting nails. She wants to get a hold of this guy and beat him to within an inch of his life. She's with her mother at the hospital, and I have placed a guard at the door. I told Melissa her mother could come stay with us when she's released. There's plenty of room."

"Do you think it was the stalker?"

"It's absolutely him, because Melissa's mom told us the questions were specifically about her and Rachael. Since he doesn't know where to look, he's picking the most likely places. It is a matter of time until he connects Melissa to me. When he does, he'll head to the cabin. Be careful. He is mean and rough. He also has a gun register to him. I think he hit Melissa's mom with it, but didn't shoot."

"When I talked to Rachael earlier, she wanted to leave. I convinced her to stay. I'll keep this part to myself until he is caught."

"Good idea. I don't have to tell you this, but don't let her go off on her own. If he goes there, he'll probably observe your routine, waiting for the opportunity to get her alone. By the way, how are things between you two?"

"Great. We manage to share duties, such as cooking and cleaning. She's easy to get along with. I haven't had to take my anti-anxiety pills for the last few days. The nightmares have subsided. The last one I had was weird. It turned into this crazy erotic dream."

"Are you sure it was a dream? Remember when she came in to wake you and you slugged her. Maybe, in that nightmare, you pulled her into bed and had sex with her. Dreams are crazy. You never know."

"That's crazy. I would know if she was in my bed. I couldn't have slept through that, could I? Anyway, she hasn't acted any different. Surely, she would either pull away or say something, wouldn't she?"

Tom took a minute to answer, "I don't know. I've never had bad nightmares or erotic dreams. Just keep her close and be vigilant."

"She'll not leave without me."

With the call completed, he thought about the discussion about dreams. Could he actually have had sex while sleeping? He'd ponder on that later. Randall thought Rachael wouldn't like feeling hemmed in, so he changed into his swim trunks.

He crossed the living room as she was opening her door. She wore blue shorts and a white bikini top. She was killing him standing there like a goddess with her blond hair in a ponytail and skimpy clothes.

Her lean body had curves in all the right places. He thought of her long shapely leg wrapped around his waist. Was that desire he saw in her eyes?

"I was coming to see if you would like to go canoeing. I need to get out in the fresh air. I'm tired of being my room." She smiled sweetly.

"Great minds think alike. I was about to ask you the same thing," he responded, returning the smile. They walked out to the shed and removed the canoe and oars.

Chapter 15

That old lady was not very helpful. Even when he smacked her, she told him nothing. He tried to beat the truth out of her. Her nosy neighbor called the cops. He heard the sirens, ran out the back door, and jumped over the fence. No one was going to stop him. He noticed a cop visiting her friend a couple of times while watching her house. He searched his car once and retrieved his name. The stalker checked in the address book and found two listed under his name. He went to the closest one and saw that Rachael's friend was staying there. He would google the other address.

Randall and Rachael rowed well together. Before heading out, they packed a lunch to spend time on the beach on the other side of the bridge. She surprised him when they finished eating, she removed her shorts to reveal white bikini bottoms to match her top. The suit left little to the imagination. She lathered sunscreen on and laid down for a little nap. He was having trouble sitting comfortably; his swimsuit bottoms were a little too tight in the groin area. He heaved off the ground, knowing distance would help the situation. He told her what he planned and strolled away with his back facing her.

When he returned, he suggested they pack up and head back. The sky darkened with the likelihood of rain coming, and he wanted to make it back to shore before the storm hit.

The rain let loose when they set the canoe in the shed. It came down heavy and hard, and neither of them wanted to run to the cabin. They stayed in the shed, waiting for the storm to weaken. Sitting in a couple of folding chairs in the corner, Randall started asking her about her writing.

"Do you research your topic? How do you pick you topic? Do you base any characters on real people?"

She answered each one. "Yes, I do research, especially on something I'm not familiar with. I do a lot of observing and when I put pieces together, a topic appears. I base minor characters loosely on real people. Remember, I've only written two books. I'm starting to gather ideas for my next one." Her methods intrigued him.

When they finished the subject of her writing, she asked him about his military career. "How long were you in? What motivated you to choose to serve? Where were you stationed?" As he discussed his career, anyone listening could tell he was passionate about it. His frustration showed about his discharge after ten years. "I feel lost, like a fish out of water. What do I do now? That is why I came here, trying to discover a new me." He saw the compassion she revealed. He wondered why she was so easy to talk to.

A sudden bang filled the air. Randall fell to the ground, moving into a fetal position. A bolt of lightning streaked through the sky with a loud crack of thunder soon to follow. He covered his head, cowering more tightly. Panic raced through him and he started to hyperventilate. He shook uncontrollably. He vaguely felt a soft body wrap around him, speaking in a low voice to him. The shaking lessened, as the storm weakened. She moved away when he tried to sit up straight. He hid his face from her. He felt ashamed to show his weakness, especially to her. Thankfully, she started talking about mundane subjects, as though nothing had happened. He took the time to get himself under control.

He heard her say, "Give it time, Randall. Don't rush into something that you might later regret. Something will spark your interest, when you least expect it." He knew she was answering his question of what to do in the future.

Taking a couple of deep breaths, he joined the conversation, letting the episode slip away. "I'm liking this private security gig I'm doing," he laughed, lightening the mood in the room. Rachael joined in the laugh. "Seriously though, do you have any idea who is fixated on you? Have you met someone that seemed strange?"

"No. I've been trying to figure out who it could be.

It all started around the time my book tour started a few weeks ago. About two days before leaving, I received the first text from an unknown sender. While I was on tour, flowers showed up at each hotel we stayed in. When I got back, the calls began. I guess he found out where I lived and installed cameras in the hall and in my place. Both facing the door."

"Nobody at the local signing stood out. Someone that might have hung around and gave you the creeps." He tried to spark a memory she might have rejected as important.

"There were of couple of guys hanging around, but they didn't do anything strange. But now that you brought it up, the book clerk kept watching me strangely. I don't know how to describe it. It was like he was checking me out, and if anyone stayed too long in front of me, he would ask them to move on. He didn't like anyone to ask me questions, even though I was more than happy to answer. When the allotted time ended, I started cleaning up. As I was leaving, he asked me out for a date. He suggested going for a cup of coffee, a drink, or maybe dinner. He started to freak me out, I turned and told him I wasn't interested and walked out with my agent and her assistant. I guess he was the only creepy one," she finished.

"Did you tell Tom about the clerk?" he asked, hoping this might be the lead they were looking for.

"No. I'd put the incident out of my mind. It wasn't until we started talking about that day the episode came back to me. He doesn't seem the type to be a stalker, but what do I know?"

"When I call Tom tonight to report in, I'll let him know. He can check on him." He cleared his throat, and said, "Thanks for before. Loud noises tend to freak me out since the accident. I hope I didn't scare you, or make you think I can't protect you. I feel foolish."

"No problem. I'll help you anytime you need a distraction. Truthfully, it could happen to anyone who had been through what you went through. You're not a fool." With a big smile, she gave him a hug.

They ran to the cabin since the rain stopped. Rachael said, "I'm going to take a shower and scribble some ideas I thought of today.

I might incorporated them in my next book. I have to come up with some basic idea, so I can outline it. Just knock on the door if you need anything."

Randall watched her sashay across the room, and what a fine sight it was.

She was tall and lean, but her slim hips swayed just a little to entice a man to watch. He wanted to follow her right into the shower. Wouldn't that be a surprise? He visualized her in her barely there suit. He loved to strip it off and wrap her long legs around him as he entered her beautiful body. That image seemed vaguely familiar to him. He considered what Tom said about his erotic dream wasn't actually a dream at all. He shook his head. How could he have sex and not know it? Rachael surely didn't act like they had sex, or if they did, it must have been unremarkable. She acted the same, except with a little more sex appeal. She was also a compassionate lady. Most woman would consider him a freak after his breakdown in the shed. Rachael had many sides, he thought. He wouldn't mind getting to know each and every one in minute detail.

He'd call Tom to let him know what Rachael had said about the clerk at her signing. She didn't give a name, but Tom could ask Melissa about the signing and go from there. He clicked on Tom's number, shaking his head to get the sexy images of Rachael in the shower out of his head.

"Hey buddy, I was just about to call you," stated Tom. "There was another break in at one of Melissa's friend's house. It looked like a twister went through it. I wouldn't normally connect the two except this friend just moved, and Melissa hadn't put the address permanently in her book. It was on a loose piece of paper stuffed in the book. The stalker might have thought that was where Rachael was hiding. Good thing Melissa's friend wasn't home. Good news from this though, he left a fingerprint. We are running it," Tom finished with a little more enthusiasm.

"This guy is relentless to find Rachael. Let's hope he doesn't connect you with her. Oh, by the way, Rachael remembered that one employee at the bookstore where she had her last signing was acting strangely. She didn't have a name, but you could check with the store manager. So far, everything is fine. I'll continue to update you and let you know if anything changes." They said goodbye and hung up.

"Any news from Tom?" asked Rachael, startling him.

He took a deep breath and said, "A friend of Melissa had her house broken into and tossed about. Thankfully, nobody was home."

"Then, I guess they haven't found him. Is this nightmare going to end? I'll head back into my room and do some more work. I think I've come up with a solid idea for my next book." She returned to her room with sagging shoulders. He wanted to cheer her up.

"Hey Rachael!" She turned around at her door. "Don't go back to your room. Let's spend some more time getting to know one another. Do you play cards? Or we could listen to soft music and talk. Please." Randall asked with a smile nobody could resist.

"Okay. Let's have some music, and I think I saw some ice cream in the freezer. We can talk over a bowl," she suggested.

"Sure. I'll put on the music, and you can dish up the ice cream."

From the kitchen, Rachael asked, "What flavor do you want? We have Rocky Road and Butter Pecan."

"I'll have Butter Pecan with some chocolate syrup." He found a smooth jazz station that was soft and sexy.

Rachael brought the two bowls of ice cream, swaying to the rhythm of the music. She handed him the one with chocolate syrup and sat on the couch with her legs crossed in yoga style.

They ate a couple of bites and he asked, "Why aren't you married? You're beautiful and intelligent. I'm surprised some guy hasn't snatched you up. Or do you have a boyfriend back in the city?"

"No boyfriend. I want to establish myself as a writer before settling down. What about you? Now that you're out of the service, will you be settling down?"

"I haven't thought about marriage. My mother has though. That is what drove me to find peace and solitude. She kept hinting about marriage and grandbabies.

"All I have on my mind is to find a job and, hopefully, get this leg a little stronger. Anyway, who would want a washed up guy like me?"

As Randall spoke, the bitterness crept in his voice.

"You're a very handsome man, and you're using your leg as an excuse. I understand that you might want a job before marrying, but you could find a girlfriend while you're establishing yourself. Any woman would be proud to have you."

"The same goes for you, sweetheart. You could date while writing your books."

"I've tried, but all a guy wants from me is to get into my bed. Thanks, but no thanks. I want something to build on." Randall knew all too well where those guys were coming from. Rachael. Bed. Dream come true.

They finished their ice cream and sat, listening to the soft music. "Would you like to dance?" he offered.

"That would be nice. If it bothers your leg, we can stop." They danced a couple of songs and then relaxed, listening to the music.

The romantic moment disappear as Rachael reached out for his bowl. When their fingers touched, he felt a spark. Their gazes met and he could see desire in hers. She broke the contact, saying, "I'm heading to bed. Thanks for the lovely evening. The dancing was a nice touch."

Chapter 16

The next morning, as Rachael was getting ready for her morning trek around the lake, she was trying to figure out ways to entice Randall. When their fingers touch the night before, she could feel their mutual attraction. It was so arousing. She thought her bikini yesterday would've been hard to resist, creating a spark between them. He didn't take the bait. I could see he was interested, but he made no advances. The storm put a damper on any further enticement. His panic attack took his mind to another time, as far away from a romantic interlude as possible. Sitting and talking last night was fun. The funny stories of their childhoods made them laugh a lot. It was nice sitting together. Maybe they'll be friends when this whole stalker thing was behind them.

By the time she was dressed and on the porch, Randall was there. She appreciated the sexy hunk of a man in his shorts and tank. He wasn't concerned about showing his scar. Each day his leg got stronger and the scar didn't detract from his awesome physique. The workout with the weights gave his arm muscles more definition. A fine specimen of a man, indeed.

Breaking into her thoughts, he asked, "Are you ready?"

She nodded and he joined her at the bottom of the steps. They conversed as they proceeded at a moderate to fast pace the first lap. Coming around the final bend, she figured he would break off and do his weight workout. Instead, he surprised her and kept walking. They slowed down to a moderate pace. There was one part around the lake that was secluded from all cabins. It would be a perfect spot for Rachael to make a move. When they got there, she asked to stop.

Halting their progress, she pretended there was something in her shoe.

Bending at the waist with her back to Randall, she took it off and shook it, putting it back on.

She saw him stare at her derriere where her shorts stretched tight. Turning around, she saw the raw desire he exhibited.

"Much better," she commented, grinning. She moved into his personal space, stood on her tiptoes, and kissed him lightly on the lips. Patiently waiting for a response, his eyes turned bright blue. A blue like the Caribbean water, she felt herself drowning in them.

He placed his palms on each side of her face and bent to kiss her, a deep kiss. Bringing her arms around his neck, she pulled him closer. He wrapped his arms around her to gather her closer still, lifting her off the ground. He rubbed his tongue along her lips, and she opened for him to enter. Their tongues began to duel. Standing there kissing for what seemed like a life time, he pulled back, and exclaimed, "Wow, you sure know how to start something."

"I was hoping you noticed that. I've been waiting for you to make the first move, but I couldn't wait any longer." She leaned against the closest tree and brought his lips back to hers. When he got closer, she wrapped her legs around him. She could feel his arousal between her legs. She rubbed against him, and he moaned never breaking the kiss. He lowered one hand to her shorts, thanking herself for wearing ones with elastic. He slipped his hand inside and touched her. Her moan got lost in the kiss. He rubbed her nub, and she began moving her hips against his hand. Her world exploded. Remembering his leg, she lowered her legs and pressed her head against his chest, taking deep breaths.

"Let's get back to the cabin and finish this. Which way is closer?" Randall inquired.

"We're more than half way, let's continue on to the end." Her lighthearted mood was infectious.

"Let's pick up the pace. Don't worry about my leg, it'll be fine. I want to be inside you, I feel no pain." Rachael laughed and together, holding hands, they moved faster, almost jogging, to finish the lap.

At the cabin, they hurried up the patio stairs. At the top, they stopped and turned toward each other.

"If you don't want to continue, I'm fine with that. I don't want to rush you." Hoping he hadn't misread her, he waited for her response. He didn't want to take another cold shower.

"Which room?" she responded with a beaming smile.

"I'll let you choose since you started this." The desire showing made her weak in the knees.

She held his hand and went to her room. Once inside, she closed the sheer curtains on the French doors. She turned and walked right into his arms. He started kissing her, with his hand moving to her breast, filling it nicely. He could feel her nipple pucker up, and he rubbed his thumb over it. She moaned. As they continue kissing, they kicked off their shoes.

He started backing up until he reached the bed. Sitting down, he lifted her shirt over her head and arms. Giving it a toss, he unhooked the front clasp to her bra and slid the straps off her shoulders. She let it slide down her arms while he filled his hands with her breasts. He took her right nipple between his thumb and forefinger and lightly squeezed. She let her head fall back, and she felt his lips around her other nipple. When he started sucking on it, she sighed with satisfaction. Shivers ran down her body. She could feel a dampness between her legs.

After a few minutes of his glorious ministrations, she said, "It's my turn." She grabbed the hem of his tank, removing it from his gorgeous torso. Dropping it, she rubbed her hand on his chest, playing with his nipples. They gazed into each other's eyes, and he put his fingers inside her shorts, guiding them past her hips and letting them slide down her long legs. She kicked them away. He had left her panties on. He squeezed her bottom, eliciting another deep moan. His right forefinger moved to her sweet spot. She was already damp and ready for another ride. He pushed the cloth aside and rubbed her slit up and down.

Pushing him back onto the bed, his finger couldn't reach. She lifted her legs onto the bed to straddle him, rubbing against his rigid member. She lifted enough for him to slip a finger inside her, and she threw her head back, asking for more.

He thrust two fingers into her channel, and pumped them in and out. She grabbed his shoulder, bringing her breast closer to his mouth. His fingers continued, while his mouth sucked her breast.

His thumb found her clit and sent her over the edge, making her scream his name. Removing his fingers, she laid her head on his shoulder, and he wrapped his arms around her. She wasn't through with him yet.

She caught her breath and knelt on the floor between his legs. Tugging on his shorts and briefs, he lifted his hips to help her remove them. His hard cock stood at attention, and she wrapped her fingers around it. He let out a hiss, as she started to stroke it. She hovered over it with her mouth, staring at him. Keeping eye contact, she lowered her mouth around the tip. His irises shined a brighter blue. She took him in her mouth as deep as she could. As she moved up, he lifted her head off him saying, "Stop honey. As good as this feels, I want to come inside you."

He sat up and helped her off her knees. He quickly grabbed his shorts and took out a foil package. She smiled, glad he came prepared. He lowered her panties, and led her to the bed. "Get on your hands and knees, babe." Once situated, he ran his tongue quickly between her legs, and kissed her sweet spot. He pushed the top half of her body down to bring her bottom higher and positioned himself between her legs. He spread the condom over his rod and guided the tip to her entrance. She was wet and ready, so he shoved his cock as deep as he could get. "Oh, you are so tight. It feels like I have gone to heaven." The next plunge was deeper, and they both moaned. He reached around her body and rubbed her nub to give her pleasure. She moved her hips and soon she was tightening around him. She found her release, but he was still rock-hard. He continued his motions, skin slapping against skin. This time, they both climax at the same time.

He slid from her and went to the bathroom to discard the condom. He came back and gathered her in his arms. "That was amazing," she said. He could only nod his head. Her head rested on his shoulder and he ran his thumb along her arm. The time slipped by. Kissing her again, he sat up and rubbed his leg. "We didn't hurt your leg, did we?"

"Heck no! It's tender, but I haven't used those muscles in that capacity since the injury. I'll be all right. I'm going to take a shower and put the pulsating stream on it." He kissed her again, got off the bed, and picked up his clothes. As he strolled out of her room, she loved the view of his tight buttocks.

She whistled, and he glanced over his shoulder, shaking his booty. Leaving the door open, she rolled to her side to continue to watch him cross the living space to his room.

Rachael fell to her back and thought about what just happened. She barely knew him; however, it felt so right. He came prepared as she fingered the extra foil package left on the bed. This gave her a pause, the first time was unprotected. She hadn't given it a thought until now. She tried to think of where she was in her cycle and thought they were safe. The nightmare happened right after her period.

Since the time of his nightmare, she had wanted him again. She still wasn't sure where whey stood. Was it a one-time thing, actually a two-time thing, or was it a start of something exciting? They didn't talk about it.

She got up and picked up her clothes and put on her robe. She waited to take her shower until he was finished. She sat and worked on outlining her new book.

Chapter 17

A friend, Bill, at the land deeds office said he would help find the cabin's location. After entering the building, the stalker located his friend's cubicle. Greeting him, the stalker told Bill he was interested in the property. He didn't want Bill to ask too many questions. Bill keyed in the address, pulled up location, printed the map, and handed it to the stalker. He acknowledged it was a great area, because he fished up there all the time. Now the stalker could find his girl and get her back. She probably needed his help. She did not appear to be the country girl type. He needed to watch out for her. The stalker gathered a few things before heading to the cabin to save her.

Rachael jumped when she heard Randall scream. She quickly rose and ran to his room. At the door, she saw him tossing and turning in bed, moving from side to side. This time was worse than the others. She didn't know if she could get close enough to wake him. He was really swinging his arms, and she didn't want to get hit again. She called his name in a soft tone while she traipsed around the bed. Trying not to scare him, she continued talking in a soft voice. Finally, he quieted down a little. She shook his shoulder, but it was to no avail. He barely moved, but the pain on his face brought her to tears.

She slid down on the bed and put her arms around him, trying to comfort him. Rachael continued to softly telling him everything was okay, he was safe. He stopped moving and the pained expression left his face. She knew she should get up and leave, but something held her there with him gathered in her arms. In time, she fell asleep also.

A couple of hours later, she woke up. They hadn't moved. She tried to take her arms from around him, but he held them still.

"Don't leave yet. This feels so comforting. Please," he pleaded. She relaxed and kept holding him.

"Sometimes, talking about it helps." Rachael attempted to get him to open up a little.

"You don't want to hear about the things I see."

"Try me. I have some pretty bad dreams myself. I dream this psycho catches me and does terrible things," she revealed.

"He's not even going to get close to you, sweetheart."

She loved hearing the endearment, but she tried again. "Now it is your turn."

Randall decided to talk. "Okay, just the highlights. I'm back at the explosion. I'm trying to find my guys. I keep calling their names, but they don't respond. I frantically search for them. This past nightmare, I found them. There were human pieces everywhere. No whole bodies. I don't know if that was the case. Nobody ever told me the shape they were in. My mind conjures up these images. Why did I get spared and they didn't?" The question was a rhetorical one. He wasn't seeking an answer. Tears streamed down his face. While he talked, he turned on his back. Rachael pulled him into her arms, placed his head on her shoulder, and let him cry. He probably never let himself grieve; he needed to cleanse the unnecessary guilt out of him.

They stayed there for what seemed like hours. His tears stopped. "I'm sorry. I don't know why I said all that. Now you'll probably have more nightmares." She felt his slight chuckle.

"You needed to let it go. There was nothing you could have done for your men. You survived because it wasn't your time. I know that is hard to grasp, but it's true. God has plans for each of us, and he still wants you to do something. You'll find out in time," she theorized.

"You're easy to talk to. I never told anyone about my nightmares of that day. This is the closest I've come. I didn't even describe them to my psychiatrist. Thank you for listening and just being here."

"That's what friends are for. I hope we're friends." She smiled at him, as he lifted his head to see her face.

"I sure hope so after our little morning delight." He chuckled when she blushed.

"How's your leg?" Rachael tried to get up, but he pulled her down and kissed her.

"My leg feels great. Let's go make lunch, before I decide to have my way with you."

She gave a flirty smile and pulled him down for another kiss. He moved his hand inside her robe and rubbed her nipple. It puckered up and he gave it a little squeeze. When he finished his shower, he'd only put on some briefs. She lowered her hand down inside them and rubbed him. He groaned and, all too quickly, she removed her hands. She slipped out bed and headed toward the door. "I need a shower. I'll meet you in the kitchen." She left with a wink.

Turning on the water, she stripped and stepped under the spray. Her mind strayed to thoughts of Randall. She really wouldn't mind if he joined her, continuing what they started. Her body responded to his slightest touch. Sex with him was awesome. It had been a long time since she's been with anyone. She'd dated, but nobody interesting enough to let in her bed. Randall, on the other hand, was a great partner. It felt like they danced to the same beat. Why had she stopped their teasing? She knew how she felt about him. Were the feelings reciprocated?

She turned off the water and grabbed a towel. She dried off and wrapped the towel around herself. Back in the bedroom, she started to get dressed. She pulled a pair panties out of the drawer, when there was a knock. Her mind occupied, she automatically opened the door. Randall saw she was only wrapped in a towel. Their eyes locked, and the tension and heat grew in the room. She took his hand and led him to the bed, dropping her undergarment on the way. He kissed her and she wrapped her arms around his neck. Her towel fell, leaving her completely naked. He grabbed her tight and deepened the kiss. Her skin tingled as it rubbed against his clothes. It made her ache to the core.

"You don't know how hard it was to not come in here and join you in the shower," he stated, pulling his t-shirt over his head.

"I've some idea." She cupped her hand around him.

She lost her sense of being in his beautiful blue orbs. One hand found her breast, rubbing his thumb on her extended nipple. Her body heated like an inferno. She unbuckled his belt, unbuttoned the shorts, and lowered the zipper. She pulled them down and kneeled in front of him. She stroked him a couple of times, licking around the tip. She placed her mouth of his head and gradually took him in. He hissed and thread his fingers in her hair, pushing himself deeper in her mouth. She slowly moved his cock in and out her mouth. The more he groaned the faster she went. She wrapped her fingers around his scrotum, and she felt it tightened as he found his release. She licked all the cum off him and sat back on her heels, giving him a coy look.

He helped her stand and kissed her. He grabbed one of her legs around his hip and they fell on the bed. He kissed under her ear, along her collar bone, down to her breast. He sucked on one, while fondling the other. He continued down to her belly button, running his tongue around and in. He knelt between her legs. He kissed each thigh, as he spread her legs. He licked her and slid his tongue inside her. He rubbed his thumb on her clit, moving his tongue in and out. She fisted her hands in the sheets and clamped her thighs around his head. His attentions never ceased until he fully pleasured her.

He climbed on the bed, and kissed her hard. He rubbed his rock-hard member against her. She opened the extra condom on the bed and rolled it over him. He stood up and pulled her body to the edge of the bed. She guided his tip to her entrance, and he thrust inside her. They both wanted hard and fast. He brought her legs to rest on his shoulders for deeper penetration. They each groaned and reached their climax together.

He lowered her legs as they both caught their breaths. He removed the condom and discarded it in the bathroom. He returned with a warm washcloth and cleaned her. When he took the cloth back to the bathroom, he grabbed his shorts. She got up and started to get dressed. Pulling his shirt over his head, he stated, "You're amazing. I can't control myself when I'm around you."

"I feel the same."

They walked arm in arm to the kitchen table, where a salad and ice tea awaited them. They ate and talked about several topics.

Everything, but what happened in the bedroom. It seemed neither wanted to talk about it. What it meant? She wondered if they would keep having sex? That was a conversation for later.

Having finished eating, they sat on the porch and enjoyed the picturesque view in silence. As if thinking as one, they reached for each other's hands.

Breaking the silence, Rachael asked, "Have you given any more thought of your future? Is this little get away helping you make sense of your life?"

He remained quiet, she didn't think he would answer. "Not yet," was his only reply.

Remaining silent, they watch squirrels running about, and bunnies hopping here and there. They saw fish jump in the water and several canoes floating in the lake. It was so tranquil, one could almost forget the bad that existed.

Randall's phone rang, breaking the quiet. He excused himself and went inside to answer it. "Hey, Tom, what's up? Is there any news on the guy at the bookstore?"

"That's the reason for the call. We talked with the manger and he didn't know anything about running people off or anything else you told me. He was too busy at the register, ringing up sales. We talked to the owner, Mr. Jones. He told us he had a stock boy that was at the signing, even though he wasn't on the schedule. He hasn't been back since that day. He gave us the name, Chet Landers, and the address he had on file. We went to the address; it was an empty lot. We checked his name in the database but nothing appeared. We're assuming his name is fake also. Mr. Jones told us he hired Chet a month before the event. The manager remembered, because that was the time he placed the advertising posters for the book signing in the store windows. The stalker must have fixated on the picture of Rachael. Be careful," Tom warned.

"The owner said that he thought the boy had some mental problems. He was just trying to help him out by giving him the job."

"This guy sounds demented. Any more break ins?"

"No. Some of Melissa's friends have noticed a strange car around their house. The description is always the same. I guess he decided to observe each house for a few hours and move on to next one. I can only speculate that he will get to my cabin's address. The sole fingerprint result came back for one, Chet Andrews. I followed up to see why his prints were in the system. He has a juvenile offense and the records are sealed. How's Rachael holding up?"

"She seems fine. She finished her book and started getting ideas for the next one. She did say she felt safe here. I don't know if it is because I'm here, or that it's far away from her problems. I'll keep my eyes open and make sure she remains safe. No one will get to her on my watch." They said goodbye and hung up.

Randall went back to the porch and reported to Rachael what Tom had to say. She wasn't thrilled that they hadn't caught this guy, but she felt glad she was here with him. She told him she was going to get some work done. He picked an action-packed movie to watch. He didn't want to fall asleep again and chance another nightmare.

Chapter 18

The stalker wondered how she could stand being stuck way out here. It's so isolated. She had nobody to help her. She needed to come back to the city so he could keep a watch on her. The stalker sensed he was lost, so he stopped at a diner to get better directions. He felt like he was driving in circles. Rachael must be going crazy being stuck out here. He'd find her and bring her back to safety. He missed her so much; he couldn't wait to see her. He'd introduce himself and tell her he'd keep her safe. The stalker wish he'd told her he was protecting her at the book signing. He was the only one who could keep her safe. While he was at the diner, he'd send her a reminder of what happens when she got him angry. He knew her email address and would send the message there.

Rachael's outline for her next book was almost finished. She wanted to send an email to Gretchen telling her the new ideas for the book. When she opened her email, she noticed a few from Unknown. She opened one and let out a scream. Randall came charging into her room.

"What's wrong?" he huffed.

She pointed at her computer screen. He saw the images of her studio. There were before and after shots of the wreckage inflicted. The message on each was, "You can't hide from me!" He closed the email and pulled her trembling body into his arms.

"It's okay, honey. They're gone. I promise he won't get near you. Come out to the living room and let's sit down." She shook so bad she couldn't move. He picked her up and carried her to the sofa. He placed her on his lap as he sat down so he could hold her tighter.

He gave her time to settle down. Finally, Rachael ceased to shake. She moved to sit next to him. "How did he get my email?" she mumbled.

"Did you have it in your bio on your book? Was in on the posters advertising the book signing?" She nodded to both questions. She'd completely forgot about that.

"Why is he doing this to me? I don't even know who he is? What could I've possibly done to him? Why won't he leave me alone?" Her voice raised in pitch with each question.

"Please calm down. Apparently, he's not all there. He's fixated on you for some reason. He believes you are his. He did ask you out, and you refused. In his crazy mind, that rejection set him off. However, he thinks he can win you over. Unfortunately, changing your number and coming here caused him to escalate his anger. They'll find and put him away. In the meantime, try to forget him. Don't open any more emails that you don't know the sender," he suggested.

They continued to watch the movie he had started. When that ended, they agreed on a comedy to lighten the mood. When the movie concluded, they settled on grilled steaks on the patio. He went outside to start it, while she prepared the steaks. She took them out to him and he placed them on the hot grill. He remained on the patio to keep a watch on the cooking, and she went inside to make a salad to go along with the steaks. She placed the salad, plates, utensils, and condiments on a tray and carried it to the outside table. The steaks were just finishing up and smelled heavenly. She brought a clean plate over for him to place them on. They sat at the table, served themselves, and began eating.

"Thank you for this afternoon. I don't know why I let this creep get to me. It's not like he knows where I am."

"I'm glad I was here for you. I enjoy helping damsels in distress," joked Randall. That made her smile, reducing the tension.

"These steaks are cooked to perfection. You amaze me with your cooking ability, why would you want me to cook?" She gave a little laugh. After enjoying a great meal, they watched the sunset from the porch. The mosquitos drove them inside.

"Do you play chess? I noticed a board on the bookshelf," she asked.

"I did a long time ago. I'm willing to give it a try. I probably will need a refresher on the moves. I'll bring it to the kitchen table."

Rachael brought a couple of sodas, joining him at the table.

"Ladies first." He waved at the set up board.

"Okay. Just to let you know, I haven't played in a long time either. I thought it would be a good way to spend the evening." Taking her focus off the board, she continued, "I like spending time with you. This provides me a break from my room."

"I like spending time with you, also. When Tom told me about the cabin and isolation, I anticipated the peace and quiet. However, I'm glad you showed up. Too much peace and quiet would have driven me crazy, allowing the horrible thoughts to take over my mind."

They played through the evening, each starting to pick up the strategies of the game. Their concentration focused on the game left little time for conversation. Rachael squeaked a win on the first game. The second, they were evenly matched. It ran quite late, and Randall conceded the game. They placed the pieces back into their spot inside the board box and replaced it on the shelf. They faced each other, neither one knew what should happen next.

Finally, Randall spoke, "As you well know, I have recurring nightmares. I'm afraid of sleeping together, getting violent, and hitting you again. Believe me when I say, I want you with me, next to me. However, I think it's wise if we sleep in our owns beds." His hands cupped her face and gave her a sweet kiss. He hugged her and turned her toward her room. "Please, go before I change my mind."

"Okay, for tonight you win. We'll take this one day at a time. Good night." Rachael turned on her heels and sauntered into her room, closing the door without a sound. Then she leaned against it for a couple of minutes, listening to him closing his door. She pushed away from the door and got ready for bed.

Chapter 19

As Randall closed his door, he called himself a fool. Who was he kidding? He wanted nothing more than to spend the night in Rachael's arms. It wasn't about the amazing sex, he wanted to hold her and be held. What would happen when they left the cabin? Would they continue to see other? He didn't even know what the future held for him. He took his medications, crawled into bed, and put all thoughts on hold. Taking a couple of breaths to relax himself, he closed his eyes.

A couple of hours later, a scream filled the night air. He sat straight up, knowing the scream didn't come from him. He went to check on Rachael. Opening the door, she yelled, "Leave me alone! Get away from me!" Her arms were shoving at some invisible object.

Going to her bedside, he spoke out, "Rachael, you having a bad dream. Wake up, honey." She slowly awakened. It crushed him to see the vulnerability staring back.

"What happened?" she asked in a small, soft voice.

"You were having a bad dream. Those pictures must have triggered it. You should be okay now. I'll leave you to go back to sleep."

"No!" she exclaimed. Grabbing his arm, she pleaded, "Please stay with me. At least until I fall back asleep. I'm still frightened." He couldn't miss the tremor in her voice and the fear shining in her eyes.

"Okay, move over so I can join you. It's easier for me on this side because of my leg," he explained. She slid over, and he joined her in bed. He gathered her in his arms with her head on his chest. He stroked her arm as they both fell asleep.

When Randall woke up the next morning, he felt a presence tight against his side. The thoughts of Rachael's screaming the previous night came back. They both found a peaceful night together. He tightened his hold on her when she snuggled closer. The closer her body huddled, his body responded. He looked on the nightstand, and there was an extra condom. He couldn't seem to control his libido around her. He rolled her to her back and kissed her awake. She lifted her hand and wrapped it around his neck. He moved his hand to her breast, cupping it. Something about this seemed vaguely familiar to him, and he pulled back. He remembered his erotic dream and wondered if it was a dream at all. She reached up and crushed her lips to his. He couldn't stop her any more than he could stop himself from breathing.

He slid his hand under her tank and cupped her breast, rubbing his thumb over her nipple. She moaned and arched her back, bringing herself closer to his hand. He released her mouth and started sucking her breast through the tank. She wiggled, causing him to get harder. He lowered his hand down between her legs. She opened her legs wider to give him better access. When he slid to finger under her panties, she nearly jumped off the bed. She responded to his every touch. Her sweet spot was dripping, and he was rock-hard. He wanted her and apparently, the feeling was mutual.

"Please, Randall, slide inside me now. I need you."

He removed their underwear. Crawling on top of her, he rubbed his cock against her. She reached down and started to stroke him. He stopped her and rolled the rubber on. He positioned himself at her entrance. "How much do you want me?" He strained to keep it together. If he didn't get inside her soon, he would surely die.

"Now. Don't make me wait. I want you so bad." The head penetrated her entrance. She moaned and said, "More, I want it all." He entered her slowly, watching her face glow, and her pupils grow larger. He grabbed her hips, keeping them still, while he continued his slow entry. He reversed direction and slid almost all the way out and she moaned. When he entered again, he shot into her so hard she climaxed. He moved in and out and built her up again. She tightened around him as she found another release. He kept moving, rubbing her nub to bring her close again and lifting one leg, penetrated further and they found ecstasy together.

He lifted off of her, discarded the condom, and brought a cloth to cleanse her. He took the cloth back to the bathroom, all the while, thinking of his dream. Something nagged at him. Yes, they had sex before, but both time wasn't initiated from lying next to each other. That's the familiar feeling he couldn't shake. Putting his boxers on, he sat at the edge of the bed with his forehead scrunched in confusion. She pulled herself in a sitting position, pulling the sheet with her. He saw alertness in her facial expression.

"Why did this feel like we had done it before? I mean we've had sex. However, the first time, you were on your hand and knees. The second, I took you while standing up. However, when we started kissing this morning, it felt oddly familiar. How is that possible?" He never mentioned his erotic dream to her.

She reached out her hand to his arm. "I should have told you before. During one of your nightmares, instead of punching me like the first time, you grabbed me down under you and started kissing me. I should've tried harder to wake you, but I got caught up in the intimacy of the moment and stopped trying. It felt so good, and I couldn't believe you stayed asleep."

"How far did I go?" he asked, angrily yanking his arm away from her hand.

"We went all the way. I'm sorry. I know it was wrong to keep it from you, but it was earth shattering for me. When you woke up the next morning, you didn't seem to remember it. Please don't be mad at me." Her eyes glistened with tears.

"I'm not mad, but you should've told me," Letting his anger go. "I thought it was some fanciful dream. Don't get me wrong, I loved the dream, but it doesn't compare to real deal. You're so wonderful in many ways. You being here has been the best thing for me. I think I may be getting a handle on my anxiety. I still get nightmares and loud noises still bother me. However, I haven't taken my anti-anxiety medication for several days. I'll still be careful when we leave, but I think I'm in control for the first time since the accident. I have you to thank for that." He lowered his head to kiss her lightly. "One other question before we move on, did we use protection?"

"No. However, I figured out later that we should be safe from pregnancy," she responded.

"If it has happened. I'll provide for you both. You must let me know," he insisted.

"I will. How about we go out to breakfast? I saw a diner not too far down the road past the mini-market. Then we can pick up some groceries on the way back. We're running low on a few items."

"Okay, I'll go get dressed."

Chapter 20

Randall left and Rachael sighed. She was glad he did not get mad at her even though she knew it was wrong to keep it from him. He's such a compassionate and caring man. He had a body like no other man she'd ever seen, and a kind heart to go with it. She placed her hand on her belly, wishing she carried his child. She would be over the moon. If they went their separate ways when they left this beautiful cabin, she'd never forget him. He would always be in her heart.

She stopped her musing, and picked a pretty sundress with sandals to wear. Finishing her morning hygiene, she dressed and was ready to go. She entered the living room as Randall came out of his room. He gave an admiring smile at her outfit and headed toward the front door. She watched him, noticing how well his snug jeans accented his tight rear. The loose blue polo shirt brought more color to his eyes. He gave a little cough, and she blushed. He'd caught her checking him out. She hurried out the door.

On mutual consent, he would drive. He helped her into his truck and saw him watch as her dress slide a little up her legs. When their eyes met, they smiled. He closed the door and headed around to the driver seat.

When they got to the diner, it was packed. He helped her out of the truck, watching the dress slide up her legs again. Opening the door for her to allow her to go in first, the waitress told them to seat themselves. Before heading to a table, they checked out the specials of the day on the chalk board by the door. They sat at their table just as the waitress came over.

"Good morning, my name is Eve," handing them each a menu. "What can I get you to drink this morning?"

"I'll have coffee with lots of cream, please," Rachael said.

"I'll have black coffee."

As they read through the menu, Eve brought two mugs and an insulated pot of coffee. She also brought plenty of cream. They placed their order, and Eve scurried off to the kitchen.

The diner seemed to be a popular place, and it appeared Eve was the only waitress. They figured it would take some time until their breakfast came. Randall poured the coffee and watched Rachael put four creams into her coffee.

"I guess you like coffee in your cream," he jested.

"Coffee is too bitter for my taste, but I need the caffeine, thus the cream. Sometimes, when I'm working late, I'll drink it plain for the extra boost."

To their surprise, Eve was back with their order in no time. Eve saw their amazed expressions and said, "Most of these people have already eaten, they're hanging around listening to the latest gossip. You folks are new. Are you staying at one of the cabins?"

"Yes. A friend, Tom Malone, lent it out to us for some rest and relaxation. We usually eat in, but we thought we would treat ourselves this morning."

"I know the Malone's. Nice people they all are. Tell them hello from Eve for me." Someone caught her attention, and she hurried off.

They ate in silence, lost in their own thoughts. Breaking the silence, he said, "Rachael, I'm sorry I didn't remember our first time. I'm still having a hard time grasping it all. I could understand about the hitting, though I'm truly sorry about that. I apologize for using you in such a way."

"Please, it's all right. I couldn't believe you didn't wake up, but I enjoyed the experience immensely. I should be the one apologizing for not letting you know right away."

Eve came back to check on them, and they asked for the bill. They each paid their part along with a tip.

Stepping out in the sunshine, they walked arm in arm to the truck. Heading toward the mini market, neither one saw the man watching them from inside the diner.

Chapter 21

A quick stop at the market, they purchased enough groceries to last a couple of days. Leaving the cabin increased the likelihood of the psycho spotting Rachael. Stowing the bags in the back of the truck, Randall noticed a car he saw earlier at the diner. Could be a coincidence, except the driver sat in the car, staring at Rachael. Leaving the parking lot, he asked her to describe the clerk at the book signing. The few details she mentioned fit the description of the man he saw watching her. Periodically, he checked the rear view mirror for anyone following.

"Is anything wrong?" she inquired. "You've glanced in the mirror several times since leaving the store."

"No, it's nothing," he lied. He didn't want to worry her needlessly. The car never appeared in his sight. They turned off at the road for the cabin and continued on.

After putting the groceries away, she asked, "Why did you ask me about the clerk? I didn't pay much attention to him. However, when Melissa and I had lunch, before coming here, I saw a man staring at me with menace. He gave me the creeps. When I was going to tell Melissa about him, he left. I thought I imagined it." Randall could tell she was getting spooked, and he was sorry he brought it up.

"I want to know what to look for if a stranger comes lurking around. There's nothing to worry about." The fear still showing, he knew how to get her mind off the subject. "Let's go for canoe ride. I'm not up for a hike with the big breakfast I ate but want to get out in the fresh air. What do you say?" Rachael knew he was hiding something, but let it go for now.

A canoe trip did sound like a good idea. "Let me change clothes. I'll join you on the dock."

He changed his jeans for shorts and went to the shed to remove the canoe and oars. By the time he placed the canoe in the water, Rachael strolled onto the dock. He helped her in, waited until she sat, and joined her. Handing her an oar, he pushed off and they started paddling. The lake was calm and quiet. In the middle of the lake, they drew in their paddles and floated along. They enjoyed the fresh air, the peacefulness, and solitude. Neither spoke, enjoying the time on the water.

Thirty minutes of floating, they started to paddle, and continued under the bridge to the small piece of land they beached at previously. He saw the tension in Rachael and wanted to help ease some. As Randall pulled the canoe up on the shore, Rachael glanced toward the cabin several times. She couldn't see it, but she wrapped her arms around her middle and swayed from foot to foot. Verifying the boat would not slip away, he went to her and turned her to face him.

"I'm not going to let anything happen to you. The chances of this guy finding us out here are remote." The tear that streamed downed her face nearly undid him. He wasn't a violent person by nature. However, if someone tried to harm those he cared about, watch out. He gathered her into his arms and gave her a hug.

"I feel safe in your arms. I want this guy stopped so I don't have to keep hiding out. Don't get me wrong. I love being at the cabin, it's the reason for being here that has shaken me up. He's ransacked three homes and put Melissa's mom in the hospital. I don't want you to be in danger."

"Rachael, I can protect myself and you. At the mini-market, I was being cautious when I asked you about the clerk. I didn't mean to upset you."

"Will you kiss me and make me forget."

"I would love nothing better."

They sat on the beach and kissed. He leaned her back and filled his hand with her breast. She pushed his hand lower.

Slipping into her shorts, he felt the dampness awaiting him. He would not deny her this pleasure. Rachael lifted her hips and removed her shorts.

Randall's mouth watered wanting to devour her. He broke the kiss and kneeled between her legs. He spread her legs wide and lowered his head to lick her. His tongue circled her clit. Rachael ran her fingers through his hair and pulled him closer to her. Sucking her nub, he sunk one finger into her tight canal.

"More," Rachael moaned.

A second finger joined the first and moved in and out, faster and faster. He nipped her clit and sucked harder. Her hips moved with the rhythm of his fingers. Her head moved side to side, her eyelids closed. Her moans grew louder. He could feel her getting close.

"Come for me, sweetheart. I want to watch as you scream my name."

She let go and screamed his name. He slowed down but kept them moving to prolong her climax. She opened her eyes, and they stared at one another. Neither wanted to break the connection. He pulled his fingers out and put them in his mouth, licking off her sweet juices.

He returned her shorts to cover her, lowered his body next to her, and gathered her in his arms. She snuggled closer and fell asleep. Randall's thoughts would not allow him to totally relax. He hoped the man he saw was not Rachael's stalker. He'd call Tom when they returned to the cabin.

A short time later, he woke Rachael up. "We should head back."

He helped her up and ambled toward the water. They pushed the canoe into the water and got in. They made their way under the bridge and took their time returning. As they neared the cabin, Randall noticed the dock in shambles. Rachael saw the destruction and turned her head with her eyebrows raised. He shrugged his shoulder. After beaching the canoe, Randall hopped out and helped her. Holding her hand, he asked her to stay with the canoe while he checked around. She squeezed his hands and nodded.

"If anything happens, get in the canoe and paddle to another dock for help as quickly as you can."

Leaving Rachael unattended went against his protective nature. However, he needed to check the dock. The scene resembled some crazy person took an axe to the wooden structure. There wouldn't be anything to determine who did the destruction. Returning to Rachael, he saw her sigh and release her arms from her around her stomach. Together, they put away the canoe and oars, locking the shed.

Heading back inside, Rachael asked, "What do you think? Did the sicko find me?" He put his arm around her shoulders and gave her a hug, offering little comfort telling by the way her body remained tense. He remained silent. He would keep a vigilant watch for any more trouble and stick close to Rachael.

"How about I cook tonight. I need the distraction. I make a great mushroom, bacon quiche. That and a salad would make a nice light dinner."

"That sounds great."

While she fixed the quiche, he tossed together the salad. They worked in comfortable silence. He wasn't going to let anything happen to her. He'd start carrying a knife in his holder around his waist when he went outside. Randall had a gun with him and decided to load it, just in case. Having finished the salad before the quiche was done, he went outside and called Tom.

"Hi," said Tom wearily. "Any developments?"

"Nothing definite, but I spotted a man at the market glaring at Rachael. I asked her for a description of the clerk, and it matched the guy. Even with your address, I didn't think he would find her. We took the canoe out for a distraction, and we were out most of the afternoon. When we came back, the dock was in ruins. He had plenty of time to destroy it. I haven't told Rachael my suspicions, but she's a smart lady."

"Don't worry about the dock. Just keep your eyes on Rachael at all times. Don't let her go out alone now that you believe he's in the area. I think it might be best to tell her, so she can be extra vigilant. I'm going to come out with my partner and check the surrounding woods. We might track him down before anything else happens. The drive will take a couple of hours. If we leave right now, it'll be dark before we get there.

"We'll wait and leave early tomorrow morning. We can be there at first light, giving us a better chance to find any signs of him. I want to catch him, and this could be our best shot." Tom sounded encouraging as they ended the call. Before heading in, He check the surrounding area carefully. He turned and saw Rachael standing at the patio door, observing him.

When he entered, she asked, "You've been acting strangely since we left the market. Is there something you should tell me?"

He put his hands up to curtail the questions. "I don't want to alarm you, but I saw a man staring at you at the store. Your description fits him to a tee. Now, with the dock destroyed, I'm positive it's him. He must've connected Tom to you through Melissa. I don't want you to go out walking by yourself. Please take extra precautions and scan your surroundings. Lock the patio door and windows. I'll do the same. I don't think he wants to hurt you, but I don't want him near you." He told her Tom's plans about him coming out to check the woods. Rachael's shoulders sagged with each word Randall said. He gathered her in his arms to comfort her. They stood there, wrapped in each other's arms, until the timer broke the spell.

"Time for dinner. I already set the table and put the salad there. I made some tea. Go ahead and sit, and I'll get the quiche."

Randall noticed her hands shaking as she carried the heavenly smelling quiche to the table. He reached out to grab the dish before it ended on the floor. Placing it on the table, he took her hands and kissed each one. He gave them a squeeze, kissed her forehead, and smiled. When he let go, she wrapped her arms around herself.

"I'm not very hungry. Do you mind if I call it an early night. I need some time alone. I'll lock everything before crawling into bed."

"You don't need to explain. Go ahead, I'll clean up. I'm here if you need me. Tom and his partner will find this sicko before he gets near you. I'm going to check outside one more time, before locking up."

Chapter 22

The stalker loved the dumbfounded expression on Rachael's face as the canoe came toward the demolished dock. Scaring her pleased him. The dock was the first of many things he planned to do. He had to get rid of that hulking guy that kept Rachael by his side. Surely, she was not involved with him. The stranger was making him angry. He's touching her, kissing her, hugging her. The stalker needed to get her away from him. She didn't belong to the stranger. Nobody could touch her but him. She was his soul mate. The stalker watched the stranger come outside to check things out. The fool made it easy for him to take him out. Hiding in the shadows of the shed, the stalker whacked the man with the 2x4 board he found. He stumbled around, but when another swing of the board connected, he crumbled to the ground. The stalker dropped the board and hurried to the cabin.

He saw the light in the far bedroom when he entered the cabin. He crossed to the door and opened it. Rachael looked up from her book and shock crossed her face. She screamed.

"How did you get in here? Where's Randall?" she stammered, throwing her book at him.

He deflected the book. "Your friend won't be joining you this evening," he sneered. "It's just you and me, like it's meant to be. We can't stay here though. So come along, I'm taking you back to where you belong." He grabbed for her, but she rolled away. He caught hold of her nightgown and ripped the shoulder, revealing her breast. "My God, you look delectable. I wish I had time now to taste you, but we must get out of here before your friend wakes up. I would hate to have to kill him."

On his second attempt, he caught her around the waist and pulled her toward him. She started screaming, so he slapped her to shut her up.

That only made her scream more. Nobody could hear her, but he had to hurry. He lifted her on his shoulder and she started striking his back with her fist. "You like it rough, do you?" He slapped her bottom hard. Every time she struck him, he smacked her.

When they got to his car, she started fighting him harder. He knew Rachael was trying to delay their departure in hopes of a rescue. The crazy man popped the trunk of the car and shoved her in. She scrambled to get out and he backhanded her. While she was dazed, he tied her hand and feet together with rope. He placed a piece of tape over her mouth. Before shutting her in, he fondled her exposed breast. She shrunk back further into the trunk, out of his reach. He slammed the trunk, started the car, and drove away.

Heading back to where he lived, he thought of the things he wanted to do to Rachael. Her breast were so creamy soft, he couldn't wait to touch her all over. However, she'd been bad. She left him and hooked up with another man. She needed to be punished. The slaps on the backside were just the beginning. He'd have to hurt her more to make her understand she belonged to him. Suddenly a thought came to him. He couldn't go back to his place, because the cops probably already knew about him. He received his biological parents' house after they died. It would take some time for the police to connect it to him. His real parents didn't love him and neither did his adopted parents. Rachael was the only one for him. With a little punishment, she'd learn to obey him. He would then lavish her with love. She'd have no choice but to love him back.

A few hours later, he reached his destination. He parked around the back behind some trees. It was closing in on midnight. There was a distance to the closest neighbor, so getting her in the house won't be a problem. He popped the trunk and saw her staring at him. She had such hatred in her eyes. He knew how to change her mind. If it took beating her into submission, he'd do it. He hoped he wouldn't have to. He grabbed her, slung her over his shoulder, and headed for the house. He found the key in a garden pot. He hadn't planned on coming here, so he wasn't prepared.

When he got her inside, her threw her on the couch. A cloud of dust filled the room. He'd go prepare a room for them and get a couple hours of sleep, while she was still bound up.

She was going to be a handful when he untied her.

Chapter 23

Randall slowly got up on his feet. He touched the back of his head and felt a sticky substance. Blood. The pounding in his head made the trip to the cabin painful. He stumbled inside only to find it empty. Rachael had been taken. He made it to his truck and noticed the slashed tire. Finding the same think on the other car, he called Tom.

"We're on our way, should be there in thirty minutes."

"Come straight to the cabin. He took Rachael, after knocking me out with a 2x4." He heard Tom slamming his hand against something, probably the steering wheel. "He slashed two tires on each of our cars, so I need you to pick me up."

"Okay, we'll come get you and head back. He surely wouldn't hurt her," he insisted.

"I don't know what his plans are, but I'm going to get there before he hurts her!"

Fifteen minutes later, Tom pulled into the drive. Randall jumped into the back seat, and they headed back down the lane. As they started back to the city, Tom asked, "Where do you think he'll take her? We found an address for him. He must know we'd have the place staked out."

"I don't know. Where else could he go?" His gut was tied in knots. He'd failed Rachael. He had to find her before something terrible happened. Tom asked his partner, Charlie, to check if there was any other listing for Chet Andrews. The miles passed away, and Randall grew more worried this guy might snap and hurt her. Damn, he couldn't even do this right.

He should've been more prepared for an ambush. He was getting rusty. If he planned on doing private security, he needed to hone his skills.

Charlie struck pay dirt. He found that Chet was adopted by the Landers. His biological parents were the Andrews, both deceased, and they left their property to Chet, their only child. He gave Tom the address, and they headed there.

About an hour later, they silently pulled to the side of the road out of sight of the house. Each of them got out and quietly closed their doors. Randall whispered, "I'll go around back."

Tom nodded and handed him a radio. The two police detectives started for the front door with their guns ready, and Randall headed for the back. He heard the knock on the front door and scrambling in the house. Tom yelled out, "Chet, give yourself up, We know you have Rachael in there. Let her go and come out with your hands up."

Randall heard the shotgun blast and radioed Tom he was going in the back way. He quickly glances in a window in the back and saw nothing. Chet must be in the front room with Rachael. Approaching the door, Charlie radioed that a shadow was moving toward the back. Thanking him for the warning, he'd have to find a place to hide. The only place to conceal himself was the side of the house.

He'd made it around the corner as a grenade was thrown out the back window. Randall scurried to the front of the house to avoid the blast. Chet used the time to escape. They all heard the car speed off.

When the grenade exploded, Randall covered his head, fighting his demons. He processed he had to overcome this and get to Rachael. Taking a few deep breaths, his mind settled and enabled him to stand up straight.

Tom and Charlie heard the explosion and kicked the door in. Randall ran in the front door following the other two. He saw her trussed up on the couch. He ran to her, removed the tape on her mouth, and untied the rope. She started rubbing her wrists. He grabbed her in a bear hug and apologized for failing her. She trembled. Charlie said the place was clear. He canceled the backup that he called for. "He used the explosion for a diversion. He went out the back to his car," Randall stated.

Rachael calmed down and eased out of Randall's grip. She sat down and sprang right back up rubbing her bottom. The men raised their brows in confusion, and she explained, "I tried to fight him. He had me slung over his shoulder. I pounded on his back. For each hit, he slapped my bottom. Needless to say, my buttocks hurt. I'm going to move around and see if I can ease the pain. What do we do now? Will he come after me again, or will he give up? He kept rambling on about how I was his soul mate, that we were meant to be together."

"He'll not get you again. I'm so sorry he got to you this time. I'll be more prepared. Do you want to go back to the cabin or to your studio? Wherever you go, I go. It's your decision."

Placing her hand on his arm, she said, "Randall, it wasn't your fault he got to me. He knows both places. We need to go somewhere he doesn't know."

"You're right." Turning to Tom, he asked, "Is there a safe house we can use? Someplace he can't track down."

Tom thought for a moment before he spoke. "Listen, I know you want to get out of sight, but we have to catch him. I don't feel right using you, Rachael, but you're our only hope. If you go back to the cabin, Charlie and I will alternate watching from the woods. The extra pair of eyes will help. What do you think?"

"I want this finished so I can pick up the pieces of my life and move on," Rachael answered.

"Okay, let's go back to the cabin. Hopefully, he'll try again, so we can trap him." Rubbing the back of his head, Randall continued, "I want a piece of him."

Tom drove them to a car rental office, because their cars were undrivable. He dropped Charlie off on the way and told Randall Charlie was heading out to the cabin and check on things. As Tom drove away, Randall took Rachael's hand. She turned her tired looking face to him and gave a weak smile.

They strode into the office and rented a nondescript sedan. They added extra insurance, not knowing what might happen in the next few days.

At the car, Randall saw her wince as she sat. "Why don't we stop at the dollar store and get a cushion of some kind." She nodded her head.

Finding a pillow for her to sit on, they headed out of the city. "Are you okay now?" Randall inquired. She glared at his smile.

Her stomach grumbled, so he stopped at a little restaurant. "I'm hungry. Let's eat before heading out to the cabin. It'll give Charlie time to scope out the area." Rachael agreed.

During the wait to be seated, Randall teased, "Oh thank goodness, they have cushioned seats." She lightly punched him in the arm.

Rachael asked, "How did you find me so quickly?"

"Tom figured he wouldn't go to his place, so his partner dug further and found that his biological parents left Chet that house. We took the chance that he would take you there. Did he say what he was going to do since he had you in his clutches?"

"He kept going on about protecting me, from you and from myself. He's thinks I'm his soul mate and we're destined to be together. He also said he'd have to punish me for allowing you to touch me. He was freaking me out. I've never been so glad to see anyone as the three of you. Thank you." Rachael's smile didn't reach her eyes.

Leaving the restaurant, they drove toward the cabin. Randall noticed she was tensing up with each mile they drove. He took her hand in his and brought it to his lips, saying, "He won't take you again. I'm sorry. He won't sucker punch me again."

She cupped her hand around his jaw and laid her head on his shoulder. "It wasn't your fault. He's crazy. I'm just glad he didn't do you serious harm. I kind of like having you around."

"I'm not going anywhere. I like being around you."

At the cabin, they got out and scanned the area. They couldn't see Charlie, but knew he was there. He'd sent a text to Randall's phone letting them know he found a nice spot with everything in view. Chet wasn't getting to Rachael again. The tires on their vehicles needed to be replaced. Tom must know someone local to call. Tomorrow, they'd figure out what to do.

Once inside the house, he locked up. While waiting for Tom that morning, he checked that all the windows were secured. It was early evening, but Rachael's fatigue showed on her face.

She confirmed it when she said, "I think I'm going to take a hot shower and crawl into bed. I didn't get much sleep last night, bouncing in the back of the car. I'm bone-tired. Thank you, again." She reached up and kissed him. He pulled her close and deepened the kiss. "Would you like to join me in the shower."

"Are you sure? You should rest."

She led the way into her bathroom. Rachael started the shower. They helped each other take off their clothes and stepped into the stream of hot water. Rachael grabbed the soap and lathered him up. He rinsed off, took the bar of soap, and lathered her, being gentle around her buttocks. She rinsed off, and shut the water off. Randall grabbed a towel and began drying her. The friction of the towel was arousing. She took the towel and began to drying him. He was running his hands over her body. He reached her breast and fondled them. He took the puckered nipple between his thumb and forefinger, giving them a little twist.

She moaned and tossed the towel aside. She placed her fingers around his cock and began stroking. He groaned and grabbed one of her legs, wrapping it around his hip. He took his other hand and rubbed between her legs. She was wet and hot. His thumb stroked her nub, and she shook.

"Take me to bed. Help get that creep out of my head. Please."

He lifted her other leg and carried her to bed. They fell together. He rolled to the side and started sliding his hand along her body. He licked her nipples and sucked one then the other. She ran her hands through his hair. He continued to fondle her breasts, as he kissed her body until he reached the apex of her hips. He widened her legs and licked her. She lifted her hips, placing her legs on his shoulders. He sucked her sweet spot, rolling his tongue around her nub. He gently nipped it and she hollered out her release. She slid her legs to the bed.

"Randall, I want you in me. Fill me up."

He answered by lifting her hips a little higher and placing his cock at her entrance. She had a condom ready for him. He sheathed himself. He was going to go slow. He wanted to saver what he almost lost.

"I want it hard and fast. I want you badly." She pushed her hips to take him in deep, to emphasize the point.

He thrust in and out, increasing the speed. She was matching him. She tightened around him with another release. He stopped moving and slowly rolled to her side, taking her with him. They were still joined. He wrapped her leg around him. He slowly rocked back and forth, until they both found their heavenly release. So sweet, so soft. He slid out, discarded his condom, and tucked her against his side. They both fell asleep.

Chapter 24

Rachael woke up and slid on top of Randall. Sometime during the night, he put the covers over their bodies. Slowly opening his eyes, she saw the raw desire. She started kissing his chest and moved to each nibble, giving each a little nip. Randall moaned, and said, "I like waking up to this."

She winked and smiled at him seductively. She continued down his body and disappeared under the covers. She proceeded down his abdomen, alternating kissing and licking. She made it to his groin area, but didn't take him in her mouth. Instead, she started stroking him and continued with the kisses and licks across his abdomen. Her strokes increased in speed making him stiff and ready to be ridden.

She removed her hands from him and straddled her legs around his hips, pushing the covers back. One hand started touching herself and the other played with her breast. He watched the sexy little minx. She rubbed her wet pussy along his engorged cock. Randall placed his cock at her entrance. She slowly slid down taking him deep. They both moaned and smiled at each other. She started rocking on him, fondling her breast with both hands. Her nipples were puckered and Randall gave them a little twist when she held them steady.

Rachael leaned down so he could put them in his mouth. He sucked them until her core ache. She increased the tempo of her hips. She threw her head back and moaned as she shattered. He placed his hands on her hips to keep her moving and he moaned with his release. He gently kiss both of her breast. She slid down next to him and placed her head on his chest over his heart. It was pounding as fast as hers.

He lightly moved his fingers up and down her back, and she release a sigh. She settled to his side and he brought the covers back over them.

A little later, Randall started tossing and turning so much, it woke Rachael. From the contortion of his face, she knew another nightmare grabbed his subconscious. She shook his shoulder and called his name. She ducked as his fist came swinging toward her. The nightmare must be a tough one. She started running her hand smoothly over his face and said, "Wake up Randall; you're just having a bad dream."

Between her quiet words and easy touch, he began to settle down. She brought his head to her shoulder and held him until he was at peace. It was predawn and she didn't think she could go back to sleep. She slipped out from under him, trying not to disturb him. Finally, out of the bed, she headed to the shower. She had the strange sensation that someone had been watching them last night. She knew it couldn't be, because either Tom or his partner were watching the property. However, she couldn't shake the feeling. Out of the shower, she dried off and realized she didn't bring any clothes in with her. Wrapping the towel around her, she made her way back into the bedroom. Glancing at the bed, she saw Randall was a awake and was staring at her like he wanted to eat her up.

"Stop that!" She strolled over to her dresser and got her garments. "Do you want take a shower here or in your room?" She inquired.

"I'll go to mine since my clothes are there." He got out of bed naked as the day he was born. Her mouth watered, but her desire to go for her hike was stronger. She missed the day before and felt a tension she needs to release. Not sexual tension, it came from the creepy feeling of being watched. As he passed by her, he grabbed her towel to wrap around his waist.

He smiled, saying, "Turnabout is fair play. You saw me naked, now it is my turn to get my view. What a gorgeous body. Sure, you don't want to climb back into bed," he teased.

"No, though it is tempting. However, here is something to remember me by." She struck a seductive pose.

His eyes widen at the sight. "I think I'll be having a cold shower, your temptress." He shook his head.

"Are you planning on walking this morning?" She nodded. "Okay, give me a chance to shower and get dressed. I'll meet you on the back porch. I don't want you to go off alone," he cautioned.

"Okay."

She knew it would take him some time; so she dressed, went to the kitchen, and started the coffee. She grabbed two power bars and stepped out back to do her stretches. Randall joined her and prepared himself for the trail. Taking the steps, they followed the pathway to the trail around the lake. She handed him a power bar. They started at a moderate pace. Still feeling uneasy, she spoke to Randall.

"Last night, I had this feeling we were being watched. I know there are men watching, but could Chet have been at my window?"

"I don't see how, but I'll talk to one of them and see if it's possible. You were probably still freaked out about the abduction, but I'll ask. I want you to feel safe," he affirmed.

They continued, picking up the pace. They made it to the secluded area. All of sudden, they heard a crack, and a tree was falling toward them. He pushed her out of the way and barely made it himself.

Randall brushed himself off, and asked, "Are you all right?" She nodded and took his hand for help up. "Let me check the crack to see if it was natural or manmade." She followed him, checking the area where the tree broke. It was a smooth cut almost through the trunk. All someone had to do was give it a push and let gravity take over.

"Someone did this deliberately. Chet was here."

"Yes, it was cut, but we don't know who did it. The distance from any cabin would allow someone to work and not be heard. Let's finish the loop and I'll check in with Tom."

Rachael started off slowly, but the madder she got, the faster she moved. She was oblivious to her surrounding, even the fact that Randall was struggling to keep up. "Hey, Rachael, honey. Please slow down. My leg can't do this fast pace. I get that you are angry. I have a punching bag in my room. You can take your frustration out on it. Okay."

Rachael slowed her speed, and they made the half lap without incident.

Rachael had worked off some of the fury, but she was still full of angry energy. "Where is that punching bag you mentioned?" she asked, eyes blazing with fire.

He showed her the bag, and she went to work on it. "Man, I don't want to get on your bad side."

Chapter 25

Randall took the opportunity to call Tom.

"What's up? I saw you guys hurrying up to the cabin. Rachael's anger radiated off her body. Did you have a fight or something?"

"No, we just had a tree that almost fell on us. It was cut most of the way through, and just needed a shove at the right time to do us harm. In the confusion, the culprit got away. Rachael is pissed. She started speed walking. I had to ask her to slow down. She's taking advantage of the punching bag to release some of her anger."

"Where did this happen? Charlie and I have been keeping our eyes peeled to the area around the cabin and deep into the woods. How did we not hear someone chopping a tree?

"It was on the other side of the lake. You couldn't have heard it from here. Also, during the hike around the lake, Rachael told me she couldn't shake the feeling we were being watched last night. Not you, someone closer. Is there a way for someone to get to her window?" Randall asked.

"Not from where we are situated. We can see every inch around the cabin, no blind spots. However, we do a perimeter check once an hour in case he is hiding in the shadows. If he'd been aware of us and knew our patterns, that could have given him the opportunity to reach the window for a quick view. He'd be gone by the time we got around. I guess we'll skip the perimeter checks to make sure you guys are covered."

"Okay. I'm not going to tell Rachael. She's mad enough as it is. We'll talk later. When do you guys switch?"

"Twelve hour shifts, nine to nine. It sucks being me. I get the day shift." Tom hung up with a laugh.

When he turned, Rachael was standing by the door with a bottle of water in her hand. She was all sweaty and her shirt clung to her skin. "What exactly aren't you going to tell me?" The heated glare she threw his way pained him.

"You heard that. Well, Tom told me that during their perimeter checks, it is possible for someone to get to your window and take a quick glance. If Chet watched their routine, he'd seize the opportunity. Don't freak out on me, we don't know for sure."

"I know for sure. He was watching us, however little time he had. We're sleeping in your room from now on. I'm not going to give this guy any opportunity to see me again. You have blinds, and we'll use them."

"Okay, as long as you agree to stay together. We'll be safer. Is the punching bag still in one piece?" he joked.

"It's nice and stable. It helped relieve some of my tension. However, if you try to hide anything from me again, I'll use you as the punching bag. How about a quick breakfast and a canoe ride?"

"That sounds good to me."

They did their normal, he cooked while she set the patio table. When she was finished, she stood watching him. He looked over his shoulder and asked, "What?"

"I'm just admiring the view." She ambled toward him and he turned to face her. Noticing the omelets were done, she moved them off the burner and moved her body, touching his from chest down. He pulled her against him and lowered his head to kiss her. As the kiss deepened, he placed his hand on her fine ass and lifted her up to the center counter. She wrapped her legs around him and he placed his hands on the sides of her head, holding her to the kiss. He was getting harder and wanted to take her right there on the counter. His phone rang, interrupting the moment. They pulled back from the kiss, both breathless. He rested his forehead on hers to get his breath when his phone rang again. He took a deep breath and answered.

"I'm giving you one chance to leave Rachael alone," said the raspy voice. "She belongs to me. If you don't leave now, I'll kill you," the voice threatened.

"Who is this? Oh let me guess. It must be psycho Chet. Rachael doesn't belong to anyone. She doesn't want to be with you. You best get moving along. The police will find you and put you in jail where you belong." There was a scream and then the phone went silent. "That was your friend," he razzed Rachael.

"How'd he gets your number? This guy is not going to quit." Just then a shot came through the kitchen window, barely missing Randall. He pulled her off the counter and dropped to the floor. His palms were sweaty, and his body tensed up. Taking a few deep breaths to keep his shit together, he quickly called Tom.

"Heard the shot, trying to locate shooter." The phone went dead. Randall took a few more deep breaths and saw the concern on Rachael face. When he didn't feel like he was going to lose it, he released the death grip he had on her hands. He apologized, but she shook it off. Randall's phone started ringing again. He checked the ID, it was Tom. He answered, "Did you find him? The shot came too close."

"No. He was gone before I got to his position. He was deep in the woods. He is good. From where he took the shot, I couldn't have hit into the house. I'm coming toward you now."

Tom walked out of the woods, and they met him outside. "Chet must've had some training. I think I'll request two people on each shift. One will patrol the perimeter, and the other will watch the cabin. He has upped his game."

"Chet called shortly before he took the shot. He threatened if I didn't leave Rachael alone, he was going to kill me. I don't know how he got my number. It's safe to say he probably has yours and monitoring it. If you're going to call in reinforcements, I wouldn't use that one." Randall was irritated and worried about keeping Rachael safe.

"I don't want to leave you guys unprotected," Tom responded.

"We were planning on taking a canoe ride after we ate. I'm not very hungry. How about you?" Rachael trembled as she shook her head.

"Let's get on the lake and stay close to the middle," she stuttered.

"Okay, you guys go canoeing. I'll drive to the mini market and call for reinforcements. I'll grab a bite to eat, so take your time." He motioned with his head for them to go inside. Taking a seat, Tom said, "I made that comment about eating in case Chet was close enough to hear. He'll think he has plenty of time. Maybe I can catch him if I hurry back. You guys stay out as long as you want."

"It'd be nice if you caught him. This whole experience would be over. We could go back to our lives." Rachael stated with a little more pep. "There are omelets on the stove. Help yourself to one. There are tortillas on the counter. You can make a breakfast burrito you could eat while driving."

"Have fun, and see you later." Tom left, taking a wrapped omelet with him.

Randall and Rachael decided to change into their bathing suits and then head for the shed. Working together, they put the canoe in the water. Randall held it for her to get in. She sat facing the back instead of her usually position. He pushed off and jumped in, causing the canoe to wobble a little. Once he took his seat, it settled down. They paddled to the middle of the lake where a small island sat. They moved to the side not facing the cabin and rested their oars on their laps.

Rachael asked, "Are you okay now? The gunshot noise must have triggered something?"

"Yeah. I'm all right. You know loud sounds, especially gunshots and explosions, make me dive for cover. I struggled for a few minutes, but I knew I had to keep it together for you. Thanks for being patient with me."

"I could tell you were struggling. I want to be there for you the same way you are here for me." Rachael reached her hand and cupped his check. He leaned into the caress and turned his head and kissed her palm.

"I know you want to get back to your life. I hope that includes me. I like having you around. You keep me leveled and centered."

He leaned in and kissed her sweetly. As it turned more passionate, the boat started to rock. Sitting back up straight, he couldn't believe every time they touch, sparks start to fly.

She whispered, "I hope you stay in my life. I feel I'd be lost without you." Today, she wore a nice one-piece suit with shorts. She wanted to get closer to Randall. "Can we go to our secluded beach?"

"It's too close to the cabin. Chet could stumble upon us, and I don't want to be caught unaware. When we're together, I want you all to myself." He moved in for a quick kiss. When he sat back, his phone rang once. "Guess Tom is back."

"We could head back and finish what we started."

"You read my mind," he said with a smile on his face.

They started to paddle around the little island and headed to the cabin. As they got closer to land, the shed exploded. Randall fell to the bottom of the canoe and covered his head, rocking back and forth. Rachael reversed the direction of the boat back to the middle of the lake. Bringing in her oar, she lowered herself and put her arms around him. Rachael whisper to him that they were safe and rocked with him.

A couple of minutes later, her words penetrated his past memories and he stopped rocking. He took some deep breaths and got back on his seat. Seeing that he was calm again, Rachael said with a tremor in her voice, "If we hadn't spent time around the island, we could have been in the shed." Randall saw the fear and could tell she was barely holding on. His losing his shit didn't help matters. If they weren't in the canoe, he would take her in his arms and comfort her.

"He's escalating dangerously. We need to put an end to this now." His phone started ringing. Not recognizing the number, he hesitated to answer. It could be Tom's partner's phone, so he answers, "Hello. Who is this?"

"Tom says to meet him on the other side of the lake. There is a dock and he'll be standing on it." The phone went dead before Randall found out who the caller was. He told Rachael what the caller said.

"It could be a trap!" He saw the fear in her eyes.

"I thought of that, or it could be legit. The call could have been brief so nobody could trace it. This Chet guy is pretty handy with all kinds of gadgets. We'll head that way but stick close to shore. If it's a trap, he would be expecting us to come from open water.

We'll sneak up to the dock. To be on the safe side, I want to switch seats with you. If it's our man, I don't want him to have his sights on you." He was worried it was a trap, but put a brave front on for Rachael's sake. They both needed to say calm to get through this.

As smoothly as possible, they switched seats and rowed toward the shore. They turned toward the other side of the lake. It was a slow process, but finally, they saw Tom on the dock. They picked up the pace. At the dock, Tom helped Rachael out of the canoe. Randall tried to get out, but a bullet hit him, knocking him in the water. Another slug hit the deck next to Tom. He quickly got his gun out and lowered to a knee, placing Rachael behind him. Squatting behind him, she checked for any sign of Randall.

"Come on. We need to get off the dock. We're sitting ducks," he whispered. She shook her head.

"I'm not going anywhere without Randall. He must be going out of mind, between the gunshots and the explosion. I don't think he'll make it on his own. Give me your gun and help Randall into the canoe. I'll point the gun at anyone coming this way. I can protect myself. I don't think Chet wants to hurt me. He wants to get me away from you guys. This might lure him out. Randall needs your help. Please." Tears were streaming down her face.

Tom handed her the gun and disappeared under the dock. He brought Randall up on the shoreline under the dock, softly letting Rachael know he found him and he was alive. He wrapped his shirt around his shoulder to stop the bleeding and put his finger to his mouth to be quiet. Hearing the exchange between Rachael and Chet, he softly told him to stay put, so he could go help Rachael. Randall weakly nodded.

Chapter 26

Rachael was scared to death. What if Randell dies? She never told him she loved him. She needed him in her life. She prayed Tom kept him safe. She kept watch on the other end of the dock, so nobody caught her off guard. She wasn't afraid to shoot Chet if he came near her. As if her thoughts conjured him up, he appeared. He started drifting toward the end of the dock.

"Stop right there Chet. Don't come any closer?" shouted Rachael. He kept moving.

"You won't shoot me. We're soul mates. We belong together. Come with me now, and I'll spare the life of the cop. I'm sure that other troublemaker is dead. I know I hit him with my perfect aim. I've also noticed he doesn't like loud noises, the little wimp. He is weak and can't protect you like I can," Chet sneered.

Rachael's hand holding the gun shook. She steadied it with her other hand. Chet stepped onto the dock. Rachael gave another warning. He didn't stop. Rachael shot at him. Following her shot were two others. Chet dropped to his knees. As his body fell forward, his gun splashed into the water. Tom came up from under the dock and checked Chet to see if he lived. He shook his head and went to Rachael, taking the gun from her shaking hands. Her eyes glazed over as the shock started to take over.

Shaking her head, Rachael stammered, "What happened to Randall? Is he still alive?"

"He's under the dock. You can go see for yourself. I'm going to call the coroner and an ambulance."

Rachael ran down the bank to get under the dock. When she saw Randall alive, she fell to the ground and started crying.

"Come here, honey. My arm finally stopped bleeding, and I don't want to move. However, I want to hold you. I hope those are tears of joy," he jested.

She went to him and examined his shoulder. She placed her hands on both sides of her face and kissed him. "I was so afraid you wouldn't survive. I love you, Randall, with all my heart. I couldn't go on without you," she cried. He wrapped his good arm around her and pulled her to him.

They stayed that way until the ambulance came. Rachael moved out of the way when the paramedics made it down the slope. They carefully placed Randall on a board to carry him up the bank to a gurney waiting for him. Rachael followed. When they put him in the ambulance, she asked if she could ride with him. Randall was calling her name, trying to get to her. To calm him down, they let her ride along. She stayed out of the way, but kept ahold of his hand. The paramedic pulled the shirt wrapped around the wound, causing the bleeding to start again. He cleaned it as best he could, put gauze on it, and wrapped it up.

It was a long ride to the hospital. Once there, they rushed him into emergency, but that was where Rachael had to stop. Tom and Melissa arrived to check on Randall's condition. Rachael and Melissa hugged. When they let go, she turned to Tom and hugged him too. "Thank you for saving him. I don't think he would have made it without you," she said.

"Randall is strong. He'll pull through all of this. He'll get his life back in order and be stronger for it. I'll need you to make a statement for the record. Randall also, when he gets on his feet," said Tom. "Tomorrow is soon enough for you to come to the station."

The doctor came to the waiting area and asked for Rachael. Tom and Melissa followed close behind her when she moved toward the doctor. His smile was reassuring. "Mr. Lewis was very luck. The bullet missed anything vital. It'll be sore and the dressing will need to be changed daily. I'd like him to stay overnight for observation. He was underwater a long time. It's just a precaution.

"If nothing unforeseen happens tonight, I'll release him in the morning. He wants to see you now. We're waiting for a room. If you'll follow me, I'll take you to see him for few moments."

Rachael followed the doctor into the emergency area. He slid a curtain aside, and Rachael strolled in with a smile on her face. Seeing the love of her life watching her with his beautiful blue eyes made that smile grow.

"I wanted to see you as soon as possible, because I needed to tell you something. I love you, Rachael Simmons. I didn't get the chance to tell you before they pulled me away. I need you in my life." She started crying again. "I hope those are happy tears." She nodded and kissed him. The nurse came in and said they were moving him to a room, and that Rachael could follow them.

"I need to let Tom and Melissa know. What room are you taking him to." The nurse told her and she squeezed Randall's hand. "I'll see you in a few minutes." She hurried back to the waiting room with the biggest smile on her face.

"You're beaming, I guess he's all right," inquired Tom.

Rachael nodded, and stated, "They're taking him to his room now. We can go see him."

"We don't need to see him if you say he's fine. Bring him to the station tomorrow to fill out his report, so this whole matter can be finished. How are you? I mean about the shooting. I know you never shot anyone before. I want to make sure you'll be okay." Tom's concern touched her heart. "I've a name of good therapist if you need to talk it out," he suggested.

"I was shaky right after the incident, but I'm so over it. I don't even want to think about it. I'm glad it's over," she said.

"Will you be coming to my house when you finish your visit with Randall?" Melissa asked. "The police brought your cars with your luggage to my place. You'll be able to bring fresh clothes for him tomorrow."

"I guess my studio is still in shambles." They both nodded. "Yeah, Melissa, thanks. I'll be there in a little bit.

"I'll visit Randall for a few hours and then come over. I need a shower and a good night sleep. Tom, could you call Randall's parents and let them know what happened."

"I certainly will. Go, be with Randall."

"I'll see you later Rachael." Tom and Melissa said their goodbyes and left the hospital. She headed up to see her love.

When she snuck in, he was dozing. She sat quietly in the chair next to the bed, trying not to disturb him. He needed his rest.

"Hello, beautiful."

She saw the love in his eyes. "Hello. How do you feel? You had a pretty hectic day."

"I'd go through it again as long as you're safe. Come here and lie next to me, so I can hold you." Rachael went to his good side and stretched out beside him. He wrapped his arm around her and kissed her head. They snuggled together and dropped off to sleep, safe in each other's arms.

Chapter 27

A few hours later, Rachael quietly stood. She kissed Randall's forehead and whispered, "I love you. See you tomorrow." She called an Uber as she headed to the main entrance. Arriving at Melissa's house, the lights were on. She knocked at the door, and Melissa was right there to open it.

"How's he doing?"

"He's getting some much-needed sleep. He has a knot on the back of his skull where Chet smacked him with a 2x4, a little fluid in his lungs from his time underwater, and a hole in his shoulder. Otherwise, he's doing great. I really need to find a bed also. I'm exhausted. Can we talk more tomorrow?"

"Of course, go right on up to your room. I left towels out for you if you want to shower. I'll see you in the morning."

Rachael dragged her weary body up the stairs and grabbed the towels for the shower. She was tired, but she knew she would sleep better if she were clean. When she finished, she crawled into bed without bothering with a nightshirt and was asleep before her head sunk into the pillow.

Rachael woke up once during the night and remember the last time she and Randall had sex, there was no condom used. She put a hand to her stomach and prayed there was a baby. If things didn't work out like she hoped they would, then she wouldn't be alone. She fell back asleep and dreamed of baby things. The next morning, Rachael stretched and missed not having Randall to wake up to. She dressed, gathered some clothes for him, and met Melissa in the kitchen.

"Oh, good, coffee," she sighed. "Do you have any cream or milk?" Melissa handed her a cup already doctored up with her cream.

"You're so thoughtful. Something smells awesome. You must've been up a while."

"It's cinnamon rolls, and it's ten o'clock. You must've been really tired. I've never known you to sleep this late. The hospital called, and they are releasing Randall at noon."

"Are you serious about the time? I have to get a move on so he'll have something to wear."

Just then, the timer went off. Melissa brought out the rolls from the oven. They smelled divine. She handed Rachael one on a napkin and wrapped one up in another. "This is for our wounded hero. Are you going to the police station from the hospital?"

"I guess that would be best. We need to get it over and done with. I'm so relieved everything is over. What is the condition of my studio?"

"Everything has been taken to the dump. It's empty except for your desk and chair. You can stay here until the place is set up again. It's no inconvenience to me. Take all the time you like."

"We'll see how things go. Thanks for the offer." Rachael finished the cup of coffee and the roll and headed to the hospital.

When she arrived, Randall was taking a shower. She left his clothes and the cinnamon roll on the bed, and she waited in the hall with his door shut.

Ten minutes later, Randall opened the door with roll in his hand, and said, "Hello, gorgeous. You're just the person I was looking for. You could've waited in the room," he said with a wink.

"Let's get you checked out and head to the police station to give our statements."

"I'm not moving another inch until you come over her and kiss me." Rachael rolled her eyes and gave him a kiss he wouldn't ever forget. It tasted sweet and oh so right.

"Now that is what I call a kiss. I have all my discharge papers. Let's go."

A man in scrubs sauntered into the room, and said, "Your transport awaits you."

"You've got to be kidding. I'm walking out of here."

"No sir, you're not. Hospital regulations state all patients leaving the hospital must be transported by wheel chair. Sorry."

Randall looked at Rachael for help. She shrugged, stating, "Hospital policy. I'll bring my car to the entrance." Kissing him on the cheek, she took a bag he was holding and hurried off.

Once loaded in the car, they headed to the police station. Tom was waiting for them. He handed each of them a piece of paper and led them into the break area. "I didn't want to put you in an interrogation room. I'm to tell you, even though the stories are the same, you're to write what you remember, not corroborate. I'll have to leave this officer in here to keep a watch on you. Sorry, it's policy."

"If I hear 'it's policy' one more time, I'm going to punch someone."

"That's all right, Tom. We understand, don't we honey. Don't mind him, he's a little cranky."

Tom nodded and left, and they wrote their statements without another word said. When they finished, they handed them to Tom.

"Thanks for closing up this matter. I'll hopefully see you both later. I'm to tell you that Melissa is making dinner for all of us."

"Okay, see you later." They waved as they left.

Making their way to Rachael's car, she told him his truck was at Melissa's. While driving to her friend's house, Randall turned to her and said, "Rachael, I love you and would like nothing better than to spend the rest of my life with you. I hope you feel the same. However, I need to find a job and get myself better. I'm going to talk to the counselor I had here at the VA. All the explosions and gunfire have triggered my anxiety. Please be patient with me," he pleaded.

"Randall, I love you and as long as it takes, I'm by your side. I don't have much of a home, just a shell of a studio where I used to write. You should spend some time with your parents and I'll stay at Melissa's for now. We'll take our time and try to find our place that we can call home. How does that sound?" She reached for his hand and squeezed it.

"Things will work out for us. You have to meet my parents. They're amazing and will make you feel welcome."

"I'll meet them, just not today. You need some time alone with them and really talk to them, explain how you're doing. You rushed off the last time and didn't spend any quality time with them. They love you and want to help, I'm sure."

At Melissa's house, Randall came in to get his duffle bag. Rachael introduced him and Melissa hugged him tightly, saying, "Thank you for keeping my friend safe. I know you didn't sign up for all the drama, but I'm glad you were there."

"There isn't anything I wouldn't do to keep Rachael safe, you have my word. I'm going to grab my duffle bag and head to my parents. I called them this morning to let them know I was coming."

When he got to the door, Melissa asked, "Please come back tonight for dinner. Invite your parents. I'll make sure there is plenty of food. It's nice to have family and friends come together."

"If you're sure you want us all, we'll be back around six."

"That'll be great. I love cooking, so the more the merrier."

Rachael walked him out to his truck and kissed him goodbye. "I hope everything is working out for my parents. When I talked to them earlier, my mom sounded happy." Kissing her one more time, he said, "I love you. I'll see you later."

Randall rolled into his parent's drive way around 3:00 p.m. He plodded up to the door and lifted his hand to knock, stopping himself as he remembered his mother told him he didn't have to knock. He entered and saw his parents on the couch, making out.

He coughed to announce his presence, and they separated so fast his dad fell off the couch. Randall chuckled.

"Randall, sorry we didn't hear your truck," his mother stammered.

"I should've knock. In my defense, you did tell me I didn't have to. I will from now on. I guess things are good with you guys." Randall grinned from one to the other.

"Very funny. Yes, things are going great. We're arranging to renew our vows," said his dad as he got himself off the floor.

"That's great. I'm happy for both of you." They all took a seat in the living room. "I hope the invitation to stay here is still open. I'm going back to counseling. There were a few incidents in my restful, peaceful place that are causing me problems. I'm also searching for a job."

"Of course, you can stay here. I'll be glad to have you home for as long as you want. What would you like for dinner? I'll need to get some groceries," stated his mom.

"Actually, we've been invited to Tom's girlfriend's house for dinner. They would really like you to come and you can meet Rachael. She got me through the rough patches."

"Okay, dinner is settled." Hugging her son, Claire said, "I'll love having you here. Your dad is being old fashion and staying at a hotel until we renew our vows," Claire gave his dad a funny grin.

"So when is the happy event?" asked Randall.

"Two weeks from today. I'd like you to be my best man. Will you son?" Randall felt the uncertainty.

"Of course, I'd be honored."

"So, tell us more about this Rachael."

"She's amazing. We've become close. I'd like to marry her, but I need a job and get control of my anxiety."

"What kind of job are thinking about?"

"I researched private security, but nobody is going to hire someone who freaks out at gunfire or loud noises," explained Randall.

"I would."

"What?"

"I've been thinking of opening a private security agency of my own. I did a lot of that in the Marines, with the dignitaries that visited. I could use your help to find more personnel. We would especially keep an eye out for any veterans looking for a job when they're discharged. I want to help them adjust back to civilian life. Your mother and I talked about it. She's going to help with the financial side. What do you think? I'd give you plenty of time for your counseling, and your lady friend," Robert explained.

"I think that's great. It's an answer to my prayers. When I see my psychiatrist, I'll let her know of our company. She might have some veterans that are struggling with acclimating to life outside the military."

For the next couple of hours, they continued making plans, trying to find the right location, and how to advertise to find clients.

At five o'clock, they put the plans aside and readied for dinner. Robert offered to drive because of Randall's shoulder injury and Randall agreed. He held the door for his mom and then jump into the back seat. He entered the address into his phone's GPS for his dad.

When they arrived, Randall introduced his parents. Claire gave Rachael a hug, and whispered, "Thank you for keeping my son grounded."

Rachael stepped back and held Claire's hands. "I'll do anything Randall needs. He protected me and worked through a lot of his struggles on his own. He is a very strong man, and I don't mean physically. You did a great job of raising him." Rachael saw the tears forming. If they fell, she would start also. They hugged again and joined the others.

Randall pulled Rachael aside. "You get more beautiful every time I lay eyes on you. I've some news.

"As you can tell my parents have patched things up, and they're going to renew their vows. I'd like you to come as my date. I'm going to be the best man."

"You're my best man." Rachael kissed his lips and gave him a big hug, being careful of his injured shoulder.

"I have other news, but I'll share that at the table with everyone else. Let's get back to the others before I take you upstairs."

Rachael laughed and led him into the dining room. He sat with other men, while the women finished preparing the meal.

Tom said, "What does everyone want to drink?" Everyone said water at one time. "That makes my job very easy."

Tom filled each glass with water, and the ladies brought out the dinner: lasagna, salad, and garlic bread.

"Lasagna, how did you know that was my favorite dish, Melissa?" asked a surprised Randall.

"Tom told me. He remembered from high school you always got lasagna on your birthday and you making the comment that it was your favorite," explained Melissa. "It may not be as good as your mom's, but I tried.

"Thank you so much. I haven't had good lasagna since I left home. Mom made it when I came home from the VA, but it jumped out of her shaking hands. It ended on the floor. It smells wonderful."

"What a waste of her hard work," said Tom.

"I'd wait until you tasted mine before saying it's good. I haven't made it in some time," Melissa cautioned.

Randall took a bit and thought he died and gone to heaven. "This is really good. It's almost as good as my mom's," he said, smiling at Claire. "Thank you again. I've a couple items of good news. The first one, my mom and dad are renewing their wedding vows." Everyone clapped, toasting the couple with water. "Also, they're starting a security agency. My dad will head it and my mom will be in charge of finances.

"They've asked me to join them. They're giving me time to work through some personal problems." He held Rachael's hand and gave it a little squeeze.

"That's wonderful. Things are working out for you. I told you something would come up for you. You'll get control of your problems, I know it."

"I start with my counseling sessions tomorrow. She had an opening and is fitting me in."

They finished eating and the guys volunteered to clean up and let the ladies relax. When they were done, they joined the ladies in the living room and continued talking. They broke off around midnight and they all said goodnight. Randall's mom and dad left him on the door step with Rachael, giving them a little privacy. He wrapped his arms around her and whispered, "You never said if you'd be my date at my parent's ceremony."

"Yes, I'll be your date. I love you and want to be with you whenever I can. If you need anything, I'm here for you." They hugged again, and Randall left with his parents.

Chapter 28

A couple of weeks later, Rachael knew she was pregnant. It was the day of Claire's and Robert's renewal ceremony. She had dinner with the Lewis' a couple of time, so she could get to know them. She would wait until after the event to tell Randall. This day belonged to his parents.

She and Randall had gone on a couple of dates, besides the dinners, and talked on the phone every evening. They discussed his counseling and the new company starting up. He helped her get a new bed up to her studio and had to christen it. She moved back and started her third book. Her agent loved the idea, and Rachael was excited about writing it.

There was a knock on her door. It was Randall picking her up for the ceremony. She met him at the door and headed to the truck.

"You look good enough to eat," he whispered as she got in the truck. She answered with a smile. She wore an emerald green dress with gold chain and earrings. The dress was little snug in the waist, but all her clothes were getting that way. He headed off to the little chapel.

"I know this is probably not the time to ask this, but would you marry me. I want to be with you always. Spending time away from you is killing me. I love you, Rachael."

"Why did you wait until we got in the truck? Yes. Yes, I'll marry you, but you are going to ask me properly after the ceremony," she informed him with a smile on her face.

"Yes, ma'am, I will. I love your sparkle when you get a little feisty." They got to the chapel and the ceremony went off without a hitch. The reception was at his parents' house.

His mom had added his dad's name to the deed, so it became their home. Rachael and Randall hired the caterers as a gift. With the best man toast finished, he asked Rachael to stroll in the garden with him. They excused themselves and made their way to the gazebo in the corner of the garden. When they got there, Rachael inhaled the lovely scent of the surrounding roses. Randall turned to her and got down on one knee.

"Rachael, my love, will you do me the honor of being my wife?" He pulled out a velvet box and opened it, showing an exquisite diamond ring. She knelt in front of him, whispered yes, and hugged him. He removed the ring and put it on her finger. A perfect fit.

"How did you know the size?" Happy tears streaming down her face.

"I had Melissa find out for me. I wanted it to fit from the start."

"I've some news for you. You're not only going to be a husband but a father as well. I love you, Randall Lewis."

"Are you sure about the baby?" When she nodded, he placed his hand on her belly, and said, "I love you, Rachael and little one."

"I had an appointment this week to confirm it. I wanted to wait for the right time to tell you. Are you happy? I mean about the baby. It's a big surprise," said Rachael.

"Yes, I hope it's a little girl as beautiful as her mother." Randall kissed her passionately.

"I would like a little boy to grow as strong and loving as his father, but, mostly, I want a healthy baby."

"Me, too."

Epilogue

8 months later

"I'm so ready for this baby to make its appearance. It's kicking me all the time," said Rachael when Randall started rubbing her back.

"What did the doctor say when you went this morning. I'm sorry I missed the appointment, but we had a new client that insisted I be there," Randall grumbled.

"The doctor said the baby could come any day now. I hope you'll be there with me. I need you there," she said with a tremor in her voice.

"Honey, they can't stop me from being right by your side. Please don't stress about it. It's not good for the baby."

"Oh, stress is just what I needed. My water just broke. We need to get to the hospital. Could you grab my bag from my closet, and then let's go. Rachael stood and waddle to the door. At the door frame, she had a tremendous pain. "I think we better start timing these contractions. Please Randall, set your timer." He set up the timer on his watch and noticed the fear in Rachael eyes.

"Easy, honey. We'll get to the hospital in time. I've got your bag, so let's go." Randall helped her to the car. It was easier to get into versus his truck. He closed the door and ran to the driver's side. He called his parents on the way.

Five minutes after the first one, Rachael had another contraction. There was still plenty of time, but he'd get her there and settled.

Randall pulled into the emergency section and ran in and explained to the registration clerk that his wife was in labor.

"The contractions are about five minutes apart." A nurse and an orderly took a wheelchair out to the car and carefully settled her in it. Her doctor had been called.

Thirty minutes later, Rachael's contractions had increased to every three minutes. Her doctor came in and checked the pelvic area. Rachael said she wanted to push, but he said it wasn't time. Randall wiped her forehead, told her to breathe, and took a hold of her hand.

Finally, it was time for the baby to come. The doctor said, "On the next contraction, push with all your might." It took three strong pushes with Randall coaching her through it.

"Congratulations. You have delivered a little boy. He has all his toes and fingers. Let us clean him up a little and then I'll have him brought to you."

"You aren't disappointed it's a little boy, are you?" Rachael asked Randall.

"I'm glad you're both fine. I love you." He kissed her forehead. "Here he comes." The nurse placed a bundle of blue in Rachael's arms and moved aside so they could visit with him.

"We never discussed names. What are we going to name him?" she questioned.

"What was your father's name? You never told me much about your parents."

"His name was William, but I don't want to use his name. How about we name him Robert Randall?"

"I think Robert William sounds better. If we have a second boy, we will use Randall for a middle name. Unless there is a reason you rather not use your dad's name," he inquired.

"No, it's just he's not here. Robert William is a good name."

She turned the blanket away from the baby's head and said, "Hello, Robert William. You're so very precious." She turned to Randall, smiling brightly. "Isn't he the cutest baby boy you've ever seen?"

"He sure is, but I think we are a little biased." He showed a short space between his thumb and forefinger.

The nurse came over to take the baby. "We're going to finish up here and take him to the nursery. When you get settled in your room, we'll bring him to you."

"I'm going to tell my parents about the baby. We'll see you in your room." He leaned down and kissed her gently. "Thank you for the most precious gift."

Randall found his parents by the nursery window. "He should be brought in any minute. We named him Robert William. Here he comes now." The nurse brought him to the window to show the proud grandparents their grandson. A few minutes later, she placed him in his warm crib.

They returned to the waiting room, waiting to be told which room Rachael was in. Claire made a quick call to Melissa to tell her of the great news. Randall gave her a smile for thinking of Rachael's friend.

Finally, a nurse came and let them know she was in 301, in the maternity ward. When they got to the room, Randall let the grandparents enter first.

"Hello, angel. You did well. You have a strong looking son just like his dad," Robert said, kissing her forehead.

"Thank you. He gets his strength from you and his dad."

"A new generation for the Lewis Security Agency," announced Claire.

"Speaking of the agency, who is running things with all of you here?" asked Rachael.

"Steven is in the office answering any phone calls, and Mike is talking to the new clients. He's explaining about you giving birth for my reason not being there. Mike is taking lead on the investigation. The client's brother is someone I served with in Afghanistan.

"Eric had written his brother, giving him my name to call if ever there was a problem. Unfortunately, Eric died in a helicopter accident, along with three others. He left a pregnant wife behind," explained Randall.

The nurse brought the baby in for Rachael to try to feed. The grandparents decided it was time to head back to the office. They would stop by to visit later. Robert motioned for Randall to follow. "Randall, take the day off and spend it with your wife and son. With this new assignment, you may have to be gone a lot. I know Rachael is aware of your ungodly hours, but this is a very emotional time for her," his father explained.

Randall shook his dad's hand and hugged his mom saying his goodbyes. "See you later. Isn't he the sweetest looking boy?"

"He sure is son. Was there any doubt? You and Rachael will make beautiful smart babies," affirmed his mother. With that they left. Randall went back into the room and watch mother and child. His love knew no end.

Thank you for reading *Protecting Rachael (A Lewis Security Agency Book)*. I would love to hear what readers think of Randall and Rachael. Please consider leaving a review.

You can also follow me on Facebook—
www.facebook.com/teresareitnauerauthor

Printed by Libri Plureos GmbH in Hamburg, Germany